3—
Avlop
m

THE LAST COCKTAIL

On the bed lay the old man, fully dressed and fast asleep.

I'm going to wake him, said Paula to herself. It's not really my business, but all the same I am going to wake him.

"Mr. Macgregor!" she called loudly.

There was no response. She took a step nearer and for the first time noticed something odd about the way he was lying. People thus resting surely did not normally hold their arms so stiffly by their sides.

Medicine, drugs, thought Paula. He used to have a chemist's shop. Somebody had mentioned that he had kept a lot of his stock when he finally retired.

Drugs combined with alcohol. A deadly cocktail. That must surely be the answer. But had he mixed it himself or had somebody else contrived it?

MORE MYSTERIES FROM THE BERKLEY PUBLISHING GROUP . . .

THE HERON CARVIC MISS SEETON MYSTERIES: Retired art teacher Miss Seeton steps in where Scotland Yard stumbles. "A most beguiling protagonist!"

—*New York Times*

by Heron Carvic

MISS SEETON SINGS
MISS SEETON DRAWS THE LINE
WITCH MISS SEETON
PICTURE MISS SEETON
ODDS ON MISS SEETON

by Hampton Charles

ADVANTAGE MISS SEETON
MISS SEETON AT THE HELM
MISS SEETON, BY APPOINTMENT

by Hamilton Crane

HANDS UP, MISS SEETON
MISS SEETON CRACKS THE CASE
MISS SEETON PAINTS THE TOWN
MISS SEETON BY MOONLIGHT
MISS SEETON ROCKS THE CRADLE
MISS SEETON GOES TO BAT
MISS SEETON PLANTS SUSPICION
STARRING MISS SEETON
MISS SEETON UNDERCOVER
MISS SEETON RULES
SOLD TO MISS SEETON

KATE SHUGAK MYSTERIES: A former D.A. solves crimes in the far Alaska north . . .

by Dana Stabenow

A COLD DAY FOR MURDER
DEAD IN THE WATER
A FATAL THAW
A COLD-BLOODED BUSINESS
PLAY WITH FIRE

INSPECTOR BANKS MYSTERIES: Award-winning British detective fiction at its finest . . . "Robinson's novels are habit-forming!" —*West Coast Review of Books*

by Peter Robinson

THE HANGING VALLEY
WEDNESDAY'S CHILD
PAST REASON HATED
FINAL ACCOUNT

CASS JAMESON MYSTERIES: Lawyer Cass Jameson seeks justice in the criminal courts of New York City in this highly acclaimed series . . . "A witty, gritty heroine."

—*New York Post*

by Carolyn Wheat

FRESH KILLS
MEAN STREAK
DEAD MAN'S THOUGHTS

SCOTLAND YARD MYSTERIES: Featuring Detective Superintendent Duncan Kincaid and his partner, Sergeant Gemma James . . . "Charming!"

—*New York Times Book Review*

by Deborah Crombie

A SHARE IN DEATH
LEAVE THE GRAVE GREEN
ALL SHALL BE WELL

JACK McMORROW MYSTERIES: The highly acclaimed series set in a Maine mill town and starring a newspaperman with a knack for crime solving . . . "Gerry Boyle is the genuine article." —Robert B. Parker

by Gerry Boyle

DEADLINE
BLOODLINE

THE CASE OF THE ANXIOUS AUNT

ANNA CLARKE

BERKLEY PRIME CRIME, NEW YORK

If you purchased this book without a cover, you should be aware that this book is stolen property. It was reported as "unsold and destroyed" to the publisher, and neither the author nor the publisher has received any payment for this "stripped book."

THE CASE OF THE ANXIOUS AUNT

A Berkley Prime Crime Book / published by arrangement with the author

PRINTING HISTORY
Berkley Prime Crime edition / May 1996

All rights reserved.
Copyright © 1996 by Anna Clarke.
This book may not be reproduced in whole or in part, by mimeograph or any other means, without permission.
For information address: The Berkley Publishing Group, 200 Madison Avenue, New York, NY 10016.

The Putnam Berkley World Wide Web site address is http://www.berkley.com

ISBN: 0-425-15311-8

Berkley Prime Crime Books are published by The Berkley Publishing Group, 200 Madison Avenue, New York, NY 10016.
The name BERKLEY PRIME CRIME and the BERKLEY PRIME CRIME design are trademarks belonging to Berkley Publishing Corporation.

PRINTED IN THE UNITED STATES OF AMERICA

10 9 8 7 6 5 4 3 2 1

1

It was the first week of the summer vacation. Paula Glenning, Professor of English Literature at the Princess Elizabeth College of the University of London, leaned back in the garden chair and contemplated the mass of rambler roses at the far end of the lawn. For a couple of novice gardeners, she decided, she and James had made good progress since they bought the huge Victorian villa in Hampstead two years ago.

She was about to say this to James when he came out from the house after answering a phone call, but was stopped by the expression on his face.

"Aunt Isobel?" she asked instead.

He nodded gloomily. "I'll have to go. It sounds urgent."

"What's the matter with her?"

"Uncle Mac is trying to poison her."

"Not again!" Paula made no attempt to conceal her impatience. "We had this only a few weeks ago."

"And it turned out to be indigestion brought on by the experiments of their temporary cook-housekeeper."

James sat down and reached for the iced coffee. It was a beautiful balmy evening. The weather looked set for many such evenings to come, and he was even more proudly pleased than Paula with the results of their efforts in the garden. "It's probably another false alarm," he said, "but I'll have to go."

"Not tonight?"

"As soon as I can summon up the energy."

Paula sat upright and put her mug on the table. "Then I'm coming too. If you want me, that is."

A glance at his face answered her question and she got up with an air of determination. "I'll be ready in ten minutes if you'll take the chairs in and lock up."

James's Great-Aunt Isobel was the younger sister of his famous grandfather, the novelist G.E. Goff. Paula calculated that she must now be well on her way to ninety, and her husband was several years younger. They had no children and James was the nearest relative.

"What is your Uncle Mac's real name?" Paula asked when they were driving away from their own little enclave and on to the main route into central London.

James had to think before replying. "Bruce. Bruce Gordon Macgregor. But everybody has always just called him 'Mac.' "

That could indicate an easy, outgoing personality, thought Paula, or it could mean that he is generally regarded as of little account. She did not say this aloud, however, because James was in a very irritable and anxious mood.

Normally they kept away from each other's family affairs. Paula's sister and brother-in-law seemed determined to find James snobbish and condescending; and James always maintained that his relations disapproved of high-flying professional females and that Paula would find them intolerable, "practically prehistoric." That he should welcome her company now was a sign of how worried he felt. Or perhaps it was exasperation. Perhaps he was afraid that he might lose his temper with the aged aunt and say, or even do, something unforgivable.

"She's just like my Grandpa," said James suddenly, as if reading her thoughts. "Totally deaf to reason or to anybody else's point of view."

"You think your Uncle Mac might really be trying to get rid of her?"

"I wouldn't be surprised if he sometimes felt like it, but I don't think it's likely. He used to be a pharmacist. Very sober and responsible. In fact he's a bloody old bore."

Paula made no comment. James might criticize his relations, but he didn't like anybody else to do so. Perhaps, in his own middle years, he was beginning to fear that he might one day become like them himself.

They drove through the quiet City of London streets and crossed the river by London Bridge.

"They live in Greenwich, don't they?" said Paula.

"Further out." James sighed. "Nearer Bromley."

The light was beginning to fade in the sky when at last they turned into Barley Avenue and drew up under the horse chestnut trees outside the gates of a big Victorian villa standing in its own grounds. It was not unlike the one where James's grandfather had lived, thought Paula. Only once had she visited the famous writer's house, and on that occasion she had been in a state of great apprehension.

She felt a little apprehensive now, as they got out of the car. The house next door, she noticed, looked very deserted and desolate, and she remarked on it.

"A crazy old woman used to live there on her own," said James. "It's been empty for ages. Must be in a filthy state."

"At least your aunt's place looks in good condition," said Paula.

"It ought to be." James spoke gloomily. "They spend a fortune on domestic help. I've got a key," he added, "but we'd better ring the bell and give Aunt Isobel a few moments to rehearse her story."

"Haven't they got a new housekeeper now?" asked Paula after a long wait.

"Yes. She seems to be very slow off the mark. Unless it's her night off. Or Aunt Isobel has already sacked her."

The door was opened at last, and Paula had her first surprise. This was no housekeeper, but neither was it the big, domineering-looking old woman that she had expected Aunt Isobel to be. Paula looked down, from her own modest height, on a tiny, fussy creature with fluffy white hair and bright blue eyes, dressed in a pale blue summer frock.

"So you are James's wife," said the old lady, taking Paula's hand in both of hers. "Why did he never let me meet you before?"

Paula didn't need James's warning glance to tell her that there was no need for Aunt Isobel to know that she and James were not married.

"Better late than never," said Paula in a voice that sounded in her own ears unpleasantly shrill and false in comparison with Aunt Isobel's sweet low tones.

"Where is Uncle Mac?" asked James rather too abruptly.

"He's gone to bed," replied Aunt Isobel, sounding faintly reproachful. "You're rather late, dear. I thought you were never coming."

James's struggle for self-control was very obvious. So that's how she operates, thought Paula. She gets her own way by making people feel guilty. Maybe Uncle Mac really is trying to poison her. She suppressed an impulse to remind the old lady that one had either to go round or go through the greater part of London to get here from Hampstead, and that they had actually done the journey in record time. Poor James. The best way to help him was to keep quiet, to listen, and to observe.

"But how could Uncle Mac get hold of arsenic?" James said as they all settled themselves in a large square room that was unexpectedly bright and uncluttered.

"No trouble at all," replied Aunt Isobel, leaning forward and speaking in very somber tones. "He brought half his chemist's shop home with him when he retired."

"But that was ages ago," protested James. "At least twenty years."

"Is it?"

The old woman frowned, looking momentarily not quite so sure of herself, and Paula became more and more convinced that the whole story had been invented to ensure that James came to see her. But no sooner had she decided this when Aunt Isobel surprised her yet again by laughing and saying, "So it was. I seem to have lost a few years. I bet you can't remember exactly when you first took up that little teaching job of yours, now can you, laddie?"

James laughed too, much to Paula's relief. "That's where you are wrong, my dear aunt. It was the year that Grandpa was awarded the Order of Merit."

"Aye, so it was. That was an easy one. But dear me." She put a hand to her forehead. "I'm forgetting my manners. You'll take a drop of whisky, James. And your good lady?"

So she does know perfectly well that we aren't married, thought Paula, as she said politely that she would prefer coffee.

Aunt Isobel stretched out a hand for the telephone, then withdrew it, saying, "Oh. I'd forgotten. It's Tuesday. Verena isn't in the house. She's down in the summer house with the G.P.'s. They meet there when the weather's fine, but they won't be much longer, if you don't mind waiting. Verena doesn't like me to go into the kitchen." Aunt Isobel reverted to her "poor little me" tone of voice. "She says the cooking and the housekeeping are her domain. Which of course they are."

Paula glanced at James, hoping he would ask the questions that she was longing to ask herself. The new housekeeper sounded rather a different sort of person from the usual browbeaten women whom Aunt Isobel chose, only to find fault with them for inefficiency and lack of initiative. It sounded as if she had this time picked somebody who could stand up to her. How long would it last?

James did not disappoint her. "G.P.'s," he said in a puzzled voice. "Is your new housekeeper a doctor?"

Aunt Isobel laughed happily. "No indeed. Verena is a most intelligent woman, far more intelligent than most general practitioners of medicine. She is an advocate of what I believe is known as alternative medicine." Aunt Isobel seemed to fumble slightly over these last words, but quickly recovered enough to add tartly, "What your Uncle Mac in his ignorance would describe as bumkum and mumbo-jumbo. Give me a hand, James," she added, leaning forward in her chair. "I'm going to fetch the coffee myself. Verena will have to forgive me if she finds out. After all, it is my house."

James helped her to rise and offered to go with her, but this caused so much agitation that he was obliged to give in. "You can fetch the whisky," she said, "from the dining room."

After they had gone, Paula got up and walked over to the large bay window, from which she could see both the front entrance and a part of the garden at the side of the house.

When James returned she said, "Did you see them, all those people coming round from the back of the house?"

James shook his head. "I wasn't looking. The G.P.'s, I suppose. Whatever they might be. What did they look like?"

"Nothing out of the ordinary. Jeans and T-shirts. Slightly unwashed, but not seriously. Mostly young."

"Male or female?" asked James as he put down the tray with the bottle and glasses.

"Difficult to tell," replied Paula. "About half and half, I should guess."

"Bisexuals?"

"No, you idiot. I meant about equal in numbers."

"I know, love. I'm sorry. And I can't tell you what this is all about because I haven't the slightest idea, except that I suspect it is the real reason for the summons. If Aunt Isobel had asked me to come and inspect Verena and her troop of whatever they are, I'd have said no, or can't it wait. Hence Uncle Mac and the poison. I thought she was being rather halfhearted about it. I doubt if she'll mention that again."

"That's a comfort anyway," said Paula.

James disagreed. "At least we'd have got the measure of her paranoia. I find Verena and her weirdos much more worrying. And Auntie is worried too. She's fascinated, but she's also scared."

"Ssh. She's coming back."

Aunt Isobel came into the room, triumphantly but rather unsteadily carrying a tray which contained two mugs of coffee and a cracked plate on which lay some very stale-looking pieces of cake.

Paula thanked her and took the coffee. It tasted horrible, and the thought of poison returned unpleasantly to her mind.

"Aunt Isobel," said James with determination after he had poured out the whisky, "who are these people who are meeting in the summer house?"

"I told you." The old woman sounded both irritated and confused. "It's a self-help group that Verena runs."

"Yes, but what is their problem? Are they drug addicts, alcoholics, some kind of phobics?"

"That's it. They are phobics. Like those people who can't go out of the house."

"Agoraphobics," said James automatically. "But they can't be that because in that case they wouldn't be here. You said they were G.P.'s. What does that stand for?"

"Phobics, of course," retorted Aunt Isobel sharply, as if she were correcting an ignorant child.

"Yes," said James patiently, "but what about the 'G'? I can think of a number of phobias, but none of them starts with a 'G.'"

"I can't always remember it myself," confessed Aunt Isobel, suddenly reverting to being a pathetic old woman, "and Verena gets so impatient with me. But I know it's something to do with old people because that's why she thought it a good idea to meet here. We're old, you know, your Uncle Mac and I, and we don't wish any harm to anybody. So they can see for themselves that there's nothing to be worried about."

James and Paula exchanged glances. This is bizarre, the glances said, and also rather disturbing.

"Dear Aunt Isobel," said James very gently, "are you trying to tell me that your housekeeper is organizing a self-help group of young people who have a phobia about old people?"

"That's it!" cried Aunt Isobel triumphantly. "I knew you'd get there in the end, James. You always were rather slow in the uptake, even as a child. Slow but sure. A bit of a plodder, your Grandpa used to say."

James looked as if he were going to explode. Paula, controlling an almost hysterical desire to laugh, decided it was time to come to his help.

"Then I suppose the 'G' must refer to 'gerontology,' the study of aging," she said calmly. "Would the group be called the Gerontophobes? Something like that?"

Aunt Isobel beamed at her. "Aren't you the clever one! We always said that James would marry brains in the end. All this chasing after glamour girls, that's what we used to say, but when it comes to the point, it's the clever one who will catch him."

Paula dared not look at James. Her fellow-feeling for him was too great. No wonder he found his great-aunt difficult to cope with. The mixture of shrewdness and senility was disconcerting, to say the least. But mixed with the exasperation was a sense of genuine alarm.

Aunt Isobel was definitely afraid for some reason or other. It was not fear of her husband. That was an old story, possibly invented in order to enliven an uneventful life. This was something new, something real, something outside her control. Verena and her gang of G.P.'s both frightened and fascinated her. Paula and James silently signaled their thoughts to each other: This needs investigating urgently, it sounds very suspicious, and something may have to be done about it.

2

Verena was big, red-haired, handsome, and in her late thirties or early forties. She greeted James and Paula warmly and apologized for not having been in the house when they arrived.

"Mrs. Mac never told me you were coming," she said to James. "Otherwise I'd have welcomed you. I've heard such a lot about you."

She looked at him appraisingly. James did likewise. Paula, turning to face Aunt Isobel, saw that the old woman was becoming very agitated, wanting to speak but seemingly unable to get the words out.

"I didn't know they were coming," she managed to say at last. "They don't often come to see me."

"We live right the other side of London," explained James, "in Hampstead. If it were nearer . . . But we had an errand in this area today, and couldn't miss the chance of coming to see my aunt, although it's rather late for a visit."

The lie came out smoothly and convincingly. Paula, still looking at the old woman, thought she seemed to relax a little. Now why, she asked herself, must the housekeeper not know that James has been sent for?

"We helped ourselves," James was adding, waving his

hand in the direction of the whisky bottle and the coffee mugs. "I'm quite at home here, as I expect my aunt has told you."

"I wanted him to wait until you were free," quavered Aunt Isobel, "but, but . . ."

She was silenced by a fit of coughing. Paula and the housekeeper looked at her anxiously; then their eyes met for a moment before Paula turned away to see James reaching for the whisky. He handed his aunt the glass and stood in front of her, shielding her from the others, while she drank. She thanked him, and added something in an exaggerated accent that Paula could not understand. He laughed and went back to his chair.

Aunt Isobel gave a final cough and spoke with much more confidence, addressing the housekeeper. "I've been trying to tell them about your work with young people, but I'm old and stupid and I don't understand these new ideas. Perhaps you could explain to my nephew and his wife about the G.P.'s."

There was a moment's pause. Verena is not pleased, thought Paula, but she's going to put on a good act.

"I gather it is concerned with building bridges between the young and the old," said James encouragingly.

"That's part of it," said Verena. "I was a social worker, you see, for some years before I decided I needed a change, and I've always enjoyed cooking and house management."

She paused to give James a chance to thank her for looking after his aunt so well, which he did. Then he added, equally politely, "So you became aware of the generation gap in your work."

"Yes, I became very concerned about the numbers of young people who were leaving homes that had become intolerable to them, often through divorce or the death of a parent. I don't know whether you have come across that sort of thing at all."

"I think I may say I have," said James. "I've been lecturing to and listening to college students for at least twenty years."

Verena's face, already brightly colored, looked as if it was trying to emulate her hair, and she started on an explanation of her activities, full of sociological jargon, that could only incite James to further courteous sarcasm.

This was getting nowhere. Paula decided to take a hand.

"What do the members of the group actually do when they meet in the summer house?" she asked.

Verena turned to her, half-gratefully, half-suspiciously. "We discuss our experiences," she said. "We exchange ideas, we try to get at the reasons why we have this problem of making contact with old people."

"The usual self-help group procedure," said Paula. "But do you have any structured program? Any targets? Any means of assessing whether your members are benefiting by their attendance at your meetings?"

"We haven't yet devised any satisfactory method of assessment," admitted Verena, "but we're working on it."

"It's difficult when it's a question of attitudes rather than a specific problem, like drugs or alcohol," remarked Paula. "Perhaps you might consult with one of those young people's groups whose aims are specifically to help the old and the disadvantaged."

"What a good idea," exclaimed Verena, almost gushing in her gratitude. "I think our next step will be to do just that. But I mustn't keep you talking, and Mrs. Mac will be wanting to go to bed, so—"

She was interrupted by the sound of the door being flung open. It knocked against a small table, and a tall vase standing on the table teetered dangerously.

"Zavvy!" cried Verena in alarmed and angry tones. "Why are you still here?"

The tall young man who stood there was neatly dressed in regulation jeans and shirt. His hair was abundant, reddish, and long, and it was caught at the nape of the neck by a wide black ribbon. He glanced round the room and then glared at Verena. It seemed to Paula, watching with great interest, that he was making a deliberate attempt to uglify a naturally rather attractive appearance.

"Because you promised me something to eat," he snapped. "One of your best veggie efforts."

The voice matched the face. A well-educated boy pretending to be working-class, thought Paula. James would have come to the same conclusion. She looked across at James, but he was gazing anxiously at his aunt, who was now leaning back in her chair with closed eyes, looking very exhausted.

"This is my son, Xavier," said Verena. "Zavvy, you haven't met Mrs. Macgregor's nephew, Professor James Goff. And Mrs. Goff."

James raised a hand in an offhand but elegant gesture of acknowledgement. Xavier, contriving a sneer, did likewise. Paula, half-resentful, half-amused at having her own title of "Professor" conferred upon James, when in fact he had not yet been thus honored himself, murmured some sort of greeting.

"So when do we eat?" Xavier turned to his mother. "How much longer are you going to be cringing around this fucking old woman?"

All eyes turned to Aunt Isobel. Verena began a feeble protest, but was quickly silenced by the old lady's raised voice.

"Young man," she cried, sitting up very straight and staring at him, "there is no fucking going on here, in spite of these modern efforts to keep people at it until they are almost in their graves."

Paula bit back a laugh. Game, set, and match to Aunt Isobel, she thought, but not a very wise move, considering how extremely vulnerable the old woman is.

Verena was protesting again, not to her son but to Aunt Isobel. "He didn't mean it, Mrs. Mac. It's just the way young people express themselves nowadays—they do so hate any kind of pretense, and—"

"Shut up, you stupid bitch!"

This time the boy's cry came straight from the heart. All trace of affectation had gone and he looked very young and frustrated and furious as he glared at his mother. Paula actually began to feel a little stir of sympathy for him, and she also began to wonder whether Verena was nothing worse than very stupid. More stupid than scheming. Perhaps she and James had misread the situation.

But Aunt Isobel had summoned James because she was worried about the housekeeper, there was surely no doubt of that, and Aunt Isobel, after her moment of triumph, was looking very bad again. James hadn't noticed, he was looking at Zavvy, and so was Verena. It was the boy himself who called out, "Hurry up, Ma. She's having another attack."

"Oh, my God!" Verena swung round. "Where's her pills? Where's her pills?"

She made a grab for Aunt Isobel's big black leather handbag, which lay on the coffee table near her chair. James made for it too. Zavvy jumped out of the way, and the two of them nearly collided.

Paula, who was standing nearest to the door, muttered to herself, "Her husband, he's a chemist," but she had only taken a few steps when an old man appeared in the doorway. He was tall and thin and his face was long and gray. He wore a crimson dressing gown. One hand was placed in a pocket, the other arm was flailing about as if he were clearing his way through a thicket as he moved forward, taking no notice of Paula's attempt to explain the situation.

James called out, "Uncle Mac!" in tones of heartfelt relief. Zavvy pulled his mother away from the stricken old woman, as the newcomer removed his hand from his pocket, extracted a small white tablet from the bottle he had been holding, and administered it to her, murmuring soothingly in a very Scottish voice.

Everyone in the room was completely silent for a full minute. James was looking anxiously at his uncle and aunt; Paula watched the housekeeper and her son. They had moved closer together, and the little spurt of genuine anger on the boy's part seemed to be over. What were they really feeling? Was it relief that the old woman seemed to be recovering? Or was it disappointment?

Had the whole scene been planned? A very old woman in a very excitable frame of mind, with a heart condition that could finish her at any moment. A very rich old woman. Who would inherit her wealth?

Suddenly it all seemed so obvious as to be unbelievable, but Paula could not help believing it. The greed for riches was a mighty driving force, and killing disguised as a natural death was a perfect solution.

But what did they plan to do about Uncle Mac, who would surely inherit his wife's estate on her death?

Paula looked across at the old man. He had a hand on his wife's wrist and he was talking to James, quietly and reassuringly. The Scottishness was now much less marked.

"She'll be all right now. Give her another ten minutes and then we'll get her to bed. No need to call the doctor, but I'd be obliged if you would stay the night. Could you do that, lad? And your good lady?"

James glanced at Paula and she nodded vigorously.

"Ah." The old man sounded relieved. It was the first sign of emotion he had shown since he came into the room. "Then we can have a little chat, you and I."

Carefully he placed Aunt Isobel's hand on the arm of her chair, gave it a little pat, and turned to Verena.

"Mrs. Keeling, would you be good enough to prepare the back room for our visitors? I don't think we shall require a meal tonight, but perhaps early morning tea would be welcome."

James answered his inquiring look with a shake of the head, and Paula, taking the hint, also declined, although in fact she would have been grateful for such a little luxury. If there was going to be a showdown with the housekeeper, however, it would be better not to have her waiting on them. In any case, she felt some reluctance to eat or drink anything that Verena had prepared.

Uncle Mac, however, seemed to be without such fears or scruples. He was now telling Verena to bring some warm milk up to Aunt Isobel's room in about half an hour's time.

"And as it is so late," he added, "your son may stay here for the night if he wishes."

"Thank you." Verena spoke softly. Paula preferred not to try to guess the woman's feelings.

Verena turned to her son. "Do you want to stay here tonight, Zavvy?"

"Christ, no. Not in this mausoleum." He stormed out of the room. The door banged behind him; the front door was slammed even louder.

Verena turned to Uncle Mac. "I'm sorry," she said, still in an unnaturally subdued voice, "but it is difficult for young people, you know, to try to adapt themselves to—"

The old man's sudden outburst made Paula jump.

"Be quiet, woman!" he roared. "Will ye stop that havering!"

Verena burst into tears and ran out of the room. Aunt Isobel gave a little moan, and murmured something that Uncle Mac, now quiet again, bent closer to hear. Then he straightened up and turned to James.

"She'd like you to go and talk to Mrs. Keeling—tell her not to be upset. Tell her that she isn't going to lose her job."

James began to protest; the old man repeated his request in a tone of voice that held a surprising degree of authority, and then bent down to his wife again when she tugged at his arm.

"Let's go," murmured Paula to James. When they were in the hall, with the sitting-room door shut behind them, she added, "Do you think he really wants you to talk to Verena? Wasn't that just to reassure Aunt Isobel?"

James admitted that this might be so, but added that in any case he wanted to go and talk to the housekeeper. He said this in the manner of somebody who was working himself up to lose his temper completely. Paula dreaded the prospect but knew that it was useless to try to stop him. They searched the house, which took a long time, but Verena was nowhere to be found. Eventually they came back to the kitchen, a large room with a window overlooking the garden at the back of the house.

"What about the summer house where Verena was having her meeting?" suggested Paula, looking out at the stretch of lawn that showed up in the lights coming from the house. "It looks as if there's a light on out there," she added.

"I suppose we'd better go and see," said James. His belligerent mood seemed to have evaporated during the fruitless search. "I'll get the flashlight from the car."

As they made their way across the lawn Paula remarked

that the grass needed cutting. "Who looks after it?" she asked.

"Uncle Mac does a little, and they get agency people in to clear up now and then."

"So what has become of all those young people who used to volunteer to help the old?" asked Paula.

"They seem to have faded out," replied James. "I don't notice much volunteering for good works among my students nowadays."

"Neither do I," grumbled Paula, who had just caught her foot painfully on a hoe lying in the grass. "Isn't that exactly typical of life today? You don't find young people helping the old, you find them sitting around in groups discussing how to improve relationships with the old. Yet another example of all talk and no action. I'm sick of our present society. I want a revolution, I want to—"

James interrupted her, at the same time switching off the flashlight. "There may be somebody in the summer house. Let's move quietly."

The building was a modern one, a large square brick structure with three sides consisting of glass, and the far side a solid wall. The room space was plentifully furnished with chairs, a sofa, and tables. On one of these stood some Coca-Cola bottles, glasses, mugs, tea and coffee pots, and the remains of sandwiches and other light refreshments.

"Has she come out to clear up?" whispered Paula.

They drew closer. "There, on the floor," said James.

Verena's bright green dress was visible between two armchairs, and so were her legs in the black tights, and the black high-heeled shoes.

"Drunk," muttered James. "Or ill? Or . . ."

"We'd better go and see," said Paula.

3

Verena was still breathing. It took only a few seconds to establish that.

"Could she possibly have got so drunk in so short a time," said Paula as she got to her feet, "or could it be a stroke? Or—or something like that," she added uncertainly, changing her mind about mentioning her suspicion that somebody else might have been involved in this situation. She could sense that James was becoming increasingly angry and resentful at being caught up in the troubles of his elderly relatives, and he would not want to face the possibility that the situation could lead to a police enquiry.

James was still kneeling beside the unconscious woman, frowning, looking around at the disorder in the summer house. "We don't know anything about her at all," he muttered, "except that she seems to be exceptionally stupid and has a loutish-looking son who probably isn't stupid at all. And she gets very red in the face. That could be a sign of heart or circulation trouble," he added more cheerfully.

"Shall I go and fetch Uncle Mac?" suggested Paula.

"No, I'll go. You don't mind waiting here?"

"Of course not," replied Paula with more confidence than she felt.

After he had gone, and she had closed the sliding glass doors behind him, she still felt very vulnerable and exposed.

The summer house was at the far end of the long lawn. Behind it and on either side were trees and large bushes. The whole area seemed to be a most inviting spot for house-breakers, but James's old uncle and aunt had made very little attempt to protect their property.

The house itself was fitted with a burglar alarm, but as far as Paula could tell, anybody could come through the front gate and round the side of the building and down to the end of the garden without being seen or heard, not to mention the possibility of climbing through the hedge from the empty house next door or climbing the wall from the other neighboring garden.

Paula found the light switches and turned off all the lights except one table lamp. That made her feel a little better. Then she pushed at the door in the solid wall at the back of the structure, and discovered a tiny washroom and a little kitchen. For a moment or two her thoughts were diverted from the present situation as she wondered how James would react to the idea of building such an annex in their garden in Hampstead. It would do for houseguests, or for a housekeeper's room if they ever decided to indulge in such a luxury; or if one or the other of them felt the need to get out of the house and retreat into splendid isolation.

Did the old couple ever use it, she wondered, or had it been made over entirely to Verena and her affairs. It would, she discovered on further investigation, be possible actually to live here. The big sofa could be turned into a bed, curtains could be drawn across the glass sides, and there were electric heaters against the inside wall.

Paula returned from her exploring to where the woman in the green dress lay motionless on the floor. It was very frustrating not to be able to do anything for her, but one had to abide by the rules: keep them warm and wait for professional help. The heat of the day was certainly lingering on in the summer house and she was still waiting. Surely James ought to be back by now, together with Uncle Mac or a doctor or both.

Paula crouched down on the floor beside Verena, but jumped up quickly when she heard the sound of footsteps on the paved area around the summer house. Then she recoiled in a mixture of disappointment and alarm when she saw that the tall man approaching was not James, but Verena's son Xavier.

"So what's new here?" he said, in quite amiable tones. Then he saw his mother and a look of supreme disgust came over his face. "Drunk again."

He pushed aside a couple of armchairs, knelt down, and grabbed the unconscious woman by the legs. "Get her to bed," he muttered. "Sleep it off."

"Stop!"

Paula's cry was so sharp that he was surprised into obeying her. "We think she could have had a stroke, or something similar," she continued more quietly.

"You a doctor?"

"No," replied Paula, "but James has gone to fetch one. He'll be back any moment now. Does your mother often get drunk?"

Xavier sat down on one of the chairs he had been pushing about, clutched his head with both hands, and muttered angrily, "I can't handle this any longer. I can't, I can't. The silly old cow."

Paula looked at him for a moment and then she glanced round the room again. Among the remains of refreshments there was no sign of any alcohol.

"Xavier," she cried impulsively, "what *is* this group about? I can't believe in that generation gap story. It's for your mother's sake, isn't it? Isn't it? You and your friends," she went on, guessing wildly but convinced that she was getting nearer to the right track, "you're trying to keep your mother off the booze, or trying to keep her out of some other trouble, or—"

Xavier jumped up suddenly, pushed Paula out of his way, and rushed towards the entrance, shouting, "Where's that fucking doctor! She could be dying."

Two men and a woman were coming across the lawn into the light that shone from the summer house. James and Uncle Mac walked on either side of a tall young woman who was carrying a black bag.

Xavier stopped dead in front of them. "Thank God," he exclaimed with a complete change of voice and manner. "It's Rose." He turned and ran back into the summer house, where Paula was now kneeling anxiously by the side of the unconscious woman.

"Not to worry," he said, touching her on the shoulder. "It's Dr. Rose Broadbent. She knows my Ma."

Paula got up hastily to make room for the doctor, who barely glanced at her, and joined the three men, who were standing in various postures of worried helplessness.

Dr. Broadbent got to her feet and beckoned to Xavier. "I'm going to call an ambulance," she said. "Is there a phone out here?"

"Over here," said Uncle Mac, indicating one of the low tables near the back wall of the summer house. "Now calm down, lad," he added, turning to Xavier, who had sat down again suddenly and was shaking his head violently from side to side. "This doesn't mean there's anything seriously wrong. We must wait and see."

"Wait and see!" shouted Xavier, raising his head and glaring at the old man. "That's all you can say! You don't know anything about it, you silly old—"

He broke off as suddenly as he had begun, buried his head in his hands, and began to sob.

Dr. Rose Broadbent returned from telephoning, looked at the others for a moment in her cool, faintly inquiring manner, and then sat down next to the boy.

"Have you been trying to cut down again?" she asked softly.

Xavier nodded without speaking.

"It won't work, you know," she said. "There's no short-cut. Come round to the surgery tomorrow morning and I'll tell you what to do."

The boy nodded again.

"Okay." She stood up and addressed Uncle Mac. "Mr. Macgregor, I don't want to disturb your wife, but I wonder whether you would allow Xavier to stay here tonight. He's in a state of shock, and I think he could use something to help him sleep."

"Of course, of course. What do you suggest?"

She mentioned a new drug that had recently come onto the market and he nodded appreciatively. The two of them then moved closer to where Verena lay, and began to talk together in low tones. James and Paula, by unspoken agreement, walked out into the garden, where they stood together for a moment on the lawn, and then both began to speak at once.

"If there's nothing more we can do here—"

The longing to return to their own home required no expression.

"But we'd better stay," went on James as they walked towards the house. "I'm really worried about Aunt Isobel."

"And we still don't know what this is all about," said Paula. "I'm wondering if the geriatric phobics stuff is some sort of facade. If Verena really is an alcoholic and Xavier really is trying to kick the drug habit—"

"Curiosity wins the day. We'll make some coffee and wait until the ambulance has arrived and then we'll get hold of Uncle Mac and make him tell us what he knows."

"Good idea," said Paula, wondering if the old man was going to be as easy to deal with as James was implying.

They settled themselves in the sitting room, heard the ambulance arrive and depart, and got up when they heard the front door shut.

James ran to the door of the sitting room. "I want to talk to you," he called out.

"I'm going to bed," said his great-uncle. "Can't it wait till tomorrow?"

"No, it can't. We won't keep you long," said James.

The old man became very Scots in his attempt to avoid them, muttering that he must go and see to the "puir wee laddie" and to his wife.

"Xavier is already asleep," said James firmly, "and so is Aunt Isobel, and I think we ought to at least wait up until we get news from the hospital about Verena. Otherwise it looks as if we just don't care."

"It would look correct then," said Uncle Mac, sitting down and helping himself to a generous measure of whisky. "I don't care in the least what happens to Mrs. Verena Keeling. The woman's a menace, but your aunt took a fancy to her. It was all that sociological jargon. Isobel never forgave her parents for not letting her go to university to study sociology."

Paula, doing rapid mental calculations, was fascinated by this glimpse into the academic aspirations of a well-to-do young woman in the years between the First and Second World Wars. But James was determined to stick to the point.

"Where did you find her? Didn't you take up references?"

"Of course we did. A titled family, and a local charity that provides for the disabled elderly. Staffed by young people who wanted to be helpful. Mrs. Verena Keeling was a treasure."

Uncle Mac made a sound like a snort and topped up his glass.

"Did you know she had an alcohol problem?" persisted James after the silence had lasted rather too long.

"Alcohol problem, alcohol problem!" exploded Uncle Mac. "Why can't you say straight out that the woman's a drunkard? What's the matter with all you young folks nowadays?" He emptied his glass and banged it down on the tray and turned to glare at James. "Everything has to be a problem! You meet a bad-tempered bastard and you call it an attitude problem. There's no problem about it. It's just human nature. Human nature that's been since the world began and nobody's ever going to change it, whatever fancy names they invent for it. Problems indeed. Problems are what you find on the pages of your algebra textbook. Or what you put into your computer to do all the hard work for you."

The old man stopped speaking suddenly, leaned back in his armchair and shut his eyes. James, looking rather anxious, got up and laid a hand on his shoulder. "Are you all right, Uncle Mac?"

"Of course I'm all right," came the sharp retort. "I don't have any 'problems.' I'm just old. Old, old."

"I'm sorry. I won't bother you any more tonight. We'll talk tomorrow. You go to bed and Paula and I will wait up."

Mr. Macgregor made no reply. James looked more and more worried, but Paula suspected that there was a bit of acting going on here. They were very wily, very calculating, both these old people. "Manipulative" was the word that came to her mind, and she smiled to herself as she thought how Uncle Mac would disapprove of that expression too. Just another aspect of human nature.

James tried again. “You’re going to need somebody to replace Verena, since she can’t possibly stay here after this, even if she isn’t ill. I really think you must let me find you a suitable housekeeper. There’s a colleague of mine who—”

He was interrupted by the ring of the telephone. Paula, who was sitting near to it, picked up the receiver.

“Yes, he’s here,” she said, and turned to Uncle Mac. “It’s Dr. Broadbent calling from the hospital.”

The old man waved her away. “You take the message. I’m tired.”

“I’m sorry,” began Paula, speaking into the phone. She was immediately interrupted by the clear, brisk voice on the other end of the line. “Don’t worry. I heard him. Would you tell him that Mrs. Verena Keeling died a short while ago without regaining consciousness. We don’t yet know the cause, but there is severe bruising on the side of the head which may have something to do with it. I’ll come and see Mr. Macgregor first thing tomorrow morning, and I’ll tell Xavier about it myself. Thank you. Goodnight.”

The line went dead. Paula turned to the old man, who was sitting sideways in his chair, leaning right over in her direction.

“I believe you heard all that,” she said accusingly.

“I believe I did,” he replied, “but maybe you’d better repeat it for the sake of young James here.”

Paula did so.

“Damn the woman!” was James’s quite violent reaction. “I suppose she’s gone and got herself murdered by one of those—”

“It’s much too soon to say yet,” broke in Paula.

“—young thugs,” he continued as if she had not spoken. “Probably that junkie son of hers.”

Paula began to protest. Several times lately James had talked in this manner, pretending—or was he pretending?—

that he was turning into a narrow-minded, middle-aged man who no longer had any understanding for the young. It irritated her, and she was determined to let him know it, but she had hardly begun to speak when she became aware of a curious sound coming from her right—where Uncle Mac was sitting. He had turned red in the face and seemed to be having some sort of coughing fit. After a couple of seconds of genuine anxiety, she realized that he was laughing.

"Sorry," he muttered, pulling out a large white linen handkerchief from his pocket and wiping his eyes. "Sorry. Just couldn't help it. Human nature. Human nature!"

He got up and slowly walked to the door. There he turned and said, "Try not to worry, Jamie lad. It's all going to sort out. And I'll think about your suggestion for a new housekeeper. Goodnight."

4

Paula could not sleep. After lying awake for a couple of hours, envying James his ability to fall asleep and remain for a long time in that condition in almost any circumstances, she decided to abandon the attempt and to go downstairs to find something to read. Thinking it very unlikely that she would want to come back to bed, she hurriedly discarded the voluminous nightdress of Aunt Isobel's that she had borrowed, and gratefully replaced it with her own clothes.

James stirred slightly in his sleep as she was shutting the door behind her, and as she stood for a moment or two on the landing, accustoming her eyes to the dimness and recalling the structure of the house, she was very conscious of the people sleeping behind the closed doors: Aunt Isobel to the right, in the main bedroom at the front of the house, and beyond it the small room, originally a dressing room, in which Uncle Mac now slept.

To the left was the landing window, through which came the faint light which would show her the way downstairs, and below the window was the main staircase. Opposite was a smaller flight of stairs leading to the upper floor, where

Verena had her bedroom and sitting room. Somewhere up there Xavier must now be sleeping, heavily sedated.

He would wake to hear the news of his mother's death.

The thought disturbed Paula. She had not taken any liking to the boy, but neither did she feel any strong aversion to him. One would need to see him in completely different circumstances, among his contemporaries, at work or at his studies, to gain an idea of what he was really like.

Paula moved slowly downstairs, pausing again when she reached the steps nearest to the window. It was not yet four in the morning, but already, on this midsummer day, she could sense the coming of dawn. She looked out towards the trees at the far end of the garden, darkly silhouetted against the pearly gray sky. Any moment now a thrush or a blackbird would begin to sing.

Paula hurried on down the stairs, anxious not to miss this magic moment. Along the hall, through the kitchen, through the scullery—that was the quickest way out to the garden. But the bolts in the back door were stiff, the lock rather complicated, and the dawn chorus was well under way when finally she stood out on the lawn.

She shut her eyes for a moment, breathing in the sweetness of the air, feeling full of life and energy in spite of the sleepless night. When she opened them again it took a few seconds before she realized that there was something unexpected out here in the garden.

It was a light in the summer house, down at the far end, not a bright light, but a glow behind the curtains. It could mean nothing, she thought as she quickened her step. The doctor, or Uncle Mac, or even the ambulance men could have pulled the curtains across and left a light burning when they took Verena away.

Or perhaps the old couple were more security conscious

than they seemed, and had installed time switches in the summer house to make it appear occupied.

This seemed the most likely explanation, but Paula could not resist a closer investigation. As she stepped onto the gravel surrounding the building, she saw that a sliding glass door was slightly open. Surely it must have been locked last night?

Paula was just about to enter the summer house when she heard the voices, one male, one female. She stepped back again and stood very still. They were speaking quietly, but were quite audible.

"I don't believe you." The female voice sounded nervous but determined. "I believe you hit her and then panicked and came running round to our place."

"But I didn't, I didn't!" The boy's voice sounded near to tears. "I've told you again and again. I never saw my mother after I left this place. Not till I came back later and found her lying there, lying there . . ."

The voice faded away. The next Paula heard was the girl saying, very fearfully, "Suppose she dies!"

"She's not going to die." The male voice, unmistakably Xavier's, sounded stronger now. "She mustn't die. Of course she won't."

"But she might. And if she does it would be murder."

There was a silence. Paula imagined the two young people staring at each other in horror. Or perhaps they were now clinging together. Or perhaps the girl had moved away, frightened for her own safety, because whether or not the boy was telling the truth, there was no doubt that he was in a highly emotional state and that there was plenty of violence in him.

At last the girl spoke. She sounded calmer now, less scared, more determined.

"I do want to help you, Zavvy, but it will be easier if I knew the truth."

"I've told you the truth. I didn't hit her."

"But you were here."

"Not until later."

There was another pause. Paula, afraid that at any moment one of them might draw back the curtains or open the sliding door, crept round to the side of the structure, where she would not immediately be seen. When she was once more able to concentrate on listening, she heard the girl say, "But you don't know how she is—have you phoned the hospital?"

"No, I'm supposed to be asleep," was the muttered reply.

"You can phone from here." The girl's voice was louder, almost angry.

Paula waited for the reply. None came, and the girl spoke once more. "Hurry up, Zavvy, let's get it over. I'll call the hospital if you'd rather not."

Again there was no response.

Daylight was coming fast, and Paula felt more and more nervous about being discovered eavesdropping. She took a step forward and called out loudly, "Is anybody there?"

The glass door was pushed back and a girl appeared. She was short and dark-haired, and dressed in tight black trousers and sweater. She stared at Paula with alarm and hostility, but did not speak.

Paula introduced herself and added calmly, "I saw the light on in the summer house and wondered what it was."

"Zavvy called me," said the girl defensively. "He wanted help. We came out here so as not to disturb anybody in the house."

"I thought he was fast asleep," said Paula. "The doctor gave him a sedative."

The girl glanced behind her, then came down the step to

join Paula. She spoke in a voice that was now more anxious than defensive.

"He didn't take the pills. He wanted to know what was happening. His mother had an accident, and he's phoning the hospital now."

She broke off suddenly, catching her breath.

"I know about it," said Paula. "I actually found his mother unconscious here. She died last night."

"Oh no!" It was a frightened, half-stifled scream.

"I think we'd better call the doctor," said Paula, pushing past her into the summer house. "Xavier will have a shock when he hears the news, and I gather that he is—"

That he is trying to break the drug habit and is in a very disturbed state of mind, was what she had meant to say, but there was no need. The boy's actions said it all. He was sitting on the arm of a chair holding the receiver and shouting into it. "Come back! You can't leave me like this. Come back. She can't be dead. She isn't dead. She can't be."

"Zavvy!" The girl ran towards him, tried to soothe him.

He pushed her away, picked up the telephone and threw it with great force against the wall. Then he slid down onto the floor and lay there on the carpet, writhing and banging his head like a child in a temper tantrum.

The girl knelt down beside him and called his name softly. Paula checked that the phone was still functioning and then hesitated. Perhaps it was too early in the morning to call Dr. Broadbent, even if she had the number. Perhaps it would be better to call Uncle Mac. Could one do so from here, or was this phone an extension from the same line?

She touched the girl on the shoulder. "We'd better get help. Will you stay with him while I go?"

The girl got to her feet. "Can't I go?"

"Do you know Mr. and Mrs. Macgregor?"

"Sort of."

This did not sound very promising.

"I think you'd better fetch my—husband," said Paula with only the slightest hesitation. "His name is James and he's in the back bedroom on the first floor. Tell him Paula sent you and it's very urgent. What's your name?"

"Bridget Wild."

"Thanks, Bridget. Don't be long."

Paula stood in the entrance and watched the girl run across the lawn. The blackbirds were still singing and the summer morning was full of bright promise. Perhaps one needed to be middle-aged, or very old or very young, to appreciate it. The teenagers were too absorbed in their own struggles to notice the wonders of nature. Reluctantly she turned to Xavier.

He was still on the floor, but sitting up now and looking around in a dazed manner. "Where's Bridget?" he asked.

"She'll be back in a minute or two," said Paula, and hurriedly went on before he could question her further. "Do they keep any tea or coffee out here? I've had no sleep and could do with some. I expect you could too."

The boy scrambled to his feet. "I'll get it. Which do you want?"

"Coffee preferably, but I'd settle for either."

He walked over to the little cloakroom, stumbling against one of the low tables on the way, and swearing under his breath. Paula, relieved that he was proving so amenable, moved over to the place where she had seen Verena lying on the floor the previous evening.

A blow to the head. That was all she knew of the cause of death. The ambulance men had thought so, the hospital spokesperson had confirmed the supposition. Further factors might come to light, but meanwhile she was curious to see whether there was any obvious cause for the blow. Apart from the possibility that Xavier had hit her. Or that somebody else had.

The armchair beside which Verena had lain had been pushed aside by the doctor and the ambulance men, but Paula could remember its former position. It stood in the angle between the fixed glass wall and the sliding glass doors, only a few inches away from them.

The chair itself had a wooden frame, not upholstered, with cushions on the seat and at the back. It was well made, quite heavy. Anybody who tripped and hit their head on one of the wooden knobs at the back would receive a very nasty bruise.

But would it be enough to render someone unconscious, enough to kill? It scarcely seemed possible, and yet head injuries were notoriously unpredictable.

Apart from the chair, there seemed to be nothing in this corner of the summer house that could have caused serious injury—no door handles, no heavy doorstops, and the floor itself was well carpeted.

Suppose Verena had received the blow somewhere else and been dragged into the position where they had found her? After all, Xavier had grabbed her legs to drag her away before Paula stopped him. This might not have been the first time he had done so. From what Paula had overheard, it sounded as if he and his mother had quarreled, and surely that would not be for the first time. In fact Paula was reluctantly beginning to believe that Zavvy had hit his mother in the course of such a quarrel last night, run away in alarm, and then returned to find Paula on the scene.

This was the most likely explanation for Verena's accident, and the boy's behavior since then seemed to bear it out. Anger, fear, grief—there had been plenty of all three. But was there also guilt? And did Dr. Rose Broadbent suspect, and would a plea of dismantled responsibility due to drug withdrawal symptoms have any validity?

Paula moved away from the corner where Verena had lain, and stood at the entrance to the summer house. Xavier seemed to have calmed down, but she nevertheless hoped that she would not be alone with him for much longer. She was relieved to see Bridget emerge from the house and run across the lawn.

"James is on the way," called the girl. "And Mr. Macgregor." She came up to Paula and stood there, panting a little. "Where's Zavvy?"

"Making coffee."

"Oh." Bridget hesitated. "He's better, then?"

"Seems to be," said Paula in an equally offhand manner.

They stood looking at each other for a moment or two, thoughtful but silent. Paula would have liked to question the girl about Zavvy, but did not want to confess her own eavesdropping. This is James's affair, she told herself. It's up to him to decide how much we get involved in it.

At last Bridget said, "I'll go and help him," and she hurried away to the back of the summer house, calling his name as she ran.

Half a minute later she was back at Paula's side. "He's not there," she muttered angrily.

"He must be there. I'd have seen him if he came out this way."

"He's not in the kitchen or the toilet, and there's nowhere else he could be," insisted Bridget.

"This is absurd." Paula walked towards the open door at the back of the building. The door to the toilet was open. Opposite, the door of the little kitchen was also open. Unwashed cups and plates were stacked in the sink, and the flex was pulled out from the electric kettle. There was no sign of any coffee-making.

"He must have got out through the window," said Bridget.

"Evidently," snapped Paula.

Bridget recoiled at her tone, but in fact Paula's anger was directed towards herself. How could she have been so careless and so stupid as not to realize that an active youngster could easily climb out of the building that way? She had noticed herself that there was a sizeable window above the sink. Why had it never occurred to her that Xavier might run away?

"I never thought he'd run away," Bridget was saying miserably. "I'm awfully sorry."

"So am I," said Paula in a much softened voice. "I really believed he was making coffee. Where d'you think he's gone?"

"I don't know."

"He doesn't live here, does he?"

Bridget shook her head.

"But he must have a place somewhere."

There was no response. Bridget's face looked sullen and closed, and by unspoken consent they moved out onto the lawn to greet James and Uncle Mac.

5

"I'm sorry," said Paula for the third or fourth time. "It never occurred to me that he might run away."

"But after what you'd overheard—"

James, too, was repeating himself. Uncle Mac had so far said very little. He looked tired and gray this morning, old and less formidable than he had the previous night. Bridget had offered to make coffee, and they could hear her moving about in the little kitchen.

"I'll have to stay here for a day or two at least," continued James, moving restlessly around the summer house and not looking at the other two, "but there's no reason why Paula should stay, is there, Uncle Mac?"

"No, no." The old man roused himself. "We can manage, Isobel and I. You've got jobs to do. We'll be all right."

"Of course you'll be all right. And of course I'm staying."

James paused beside Uncle Mac's chair and put a hand on his shoulder. "But there's no need for Paula to. And somebody's got to feed the cats and take in the mail."

Paula got up and stood in the entrance to the summer house, looking out into the garden. If she and James had been alone they would by now have been deep in one of their quarrels. She stared at the trees and the climbing roses and the brilliant summer sky, and said nothing. It had been a great mistake to come here at all. Usually she kept clear of James's family problems. But he had wanted her to come, she reminded herself; he had been most relieved when she suggested it.

"We'll have to find you another housekeeper," James was saying. "What about that woman who used to help with my grandfather?"

Paula remained with her back to them. She was indeed longing to go home, but it must be on her own terms and of her own volition. She was not going to be sent away like a naughty child who had been meddling in somebody else's affairs. She and James must deal with this tension between them now. Otherwise it would mount and mount and there would be a knot that would take a long time to unravel.

She turned round abruptly, full of this resolution, but James was no longer there. Only Uncle Mac was there, looking up at her with tired old eyes that seemed to see a lot and not much like what they saw.

"Do you want James?" he said. "He's in the kitchen talking to Bridget."

Paula took a step in that direction and then paused.

"Do you want to go home?" asked Uncle Mac.

"I do indeed," she replied.

"Then be off with you. The police will know where to find you if they need to question you, and I'll tell Jamie."

Paula thanked him and ran off before she could change her mind.

It was strange, she thought as she hurriedly collected her purse and the jacket she had been wearing last evening, that she didn't resent this peremptory dismissal but was actually grateful for it. After all, it would not have been a good idea to have a row with James here in his relations' house, where there was trouble enough already.

The feeling of relief was only partially dented by the recollection that they had come in James's car, and that she would have to find the nearest bus or underground station.

Or phone for a taxi.

She was standing on the front doorstep, examining the money that she had with her, when Bridget appeared, very out of breath, from round the side of the house.

"Can I give you a lift?" she asked.

Paula looked doubtful.

"I've only got an ancient mini," continued the girl, "but it'll get us to the station."

"That's very kind of you. I don't know this district at all," Paula added as they came through the front gate.

"You can get to London Bridge Station."

"That'll be fine. I'm most grateful."

When they were seated in the little car Bridget said, awkwardly, "Actually I'd hoped to talk to you. I don't suppose you've got time, though."

"I'm in no hurry, but I'd rather like some breakfast. Or at any rate some coffee. Is there anywhere round here?"

"We could go to my grandfather's. That's where I live. It's not far, but it's not very . . ."

Paula interrupted the coming apology. "That makes another one."

"Another one? What d'you mean?"

"Another person who lives with or has been brought up by grandparents," explained Paula. "I was myself, and so was James, and we keep coming across more and more. It's become a sort of game with us, counting them. Isn't it silly?"

Bridget, who had only just succeeded in getting the engine to start, turned to Paula with an air of genuine friendliness and amusement.

"I don't think it's all that silly. I shall start doing it too. Do you think it would run to a Ph.D. thesis?"

"Why not, if you treat it with sufficient sociological gravity. People have written theses on much sillier subjects. Which college are you at?"

"Nowhere at the moment. I did my sociology degree at Sussex, and I'd like to do a higher degree."

Paula made suitable inquiries and gave some useful advice. By the time they arrived at a street of small terraced houses at least three social classes lower than the one they had come from, Paula and Bridget were on very friendly terms.

"My grandfather is rather eccentric," explained Bridget as they drew up outside a little greengrocer's shop near the corner. "He's been a widower for years. Everybody else died or ran away or something and we've only got each other."

"Is this his shop?"

"Yes, and I wish he'd give it up. He doesn't really need it and it hardly makes any money because he doesn't look after the business properly. Actually he's quite a successful artist—Christmas cards and posters and things—but he likes to pretend he's just a poor old thing. His name's Nicholas. I do hope you'll like him," added the girl with a return to her anxious manner.

Paula felt sure that she would. She was beginning to like Bridget, and Nicholas Wild sounded interestingly eccentric.

They came into the shop and found him unpacking a container of grapes. It was a very slow business because he was amusing himself by piling up the fruit into a pagoda-shaped structure that was clearly going to crumple up at the slightest vibration.

Paula, trying too hard to avoid bringing about this collapse, tripped over a crate of apples that was blocking the way, knocked her ankle painfully, and might have fallen if Bridget and her grandfather had not caught hold of her.

"Arnica!" exclaimed Nicholas Wild in a deep bass voice. "That's the thing for bruises. We must look after your friend, Biddy."

Paula protested that she was all right and didn't need any remedies, and Bridget began to scold her grandfather.

"Look out, you're treading on the grapes!" She knelt down and tried to salvage them. "Oh Grandpa, you are hopeless—hopeless. What am I going to do with you?"

The old man took no notice of her. He had taken Paula's hand and was apologizing for such a discourteous reception.

"You'll never get the shop open by nine," said Bridget despairingly.

"Then let them buy elsewhere," said Nicholas. "I want my breakfast. Will you join us, madam?"

Paula gave her name.

"She's a university professor," cried Bridget, following the two of them to a door that led into a narrow corridor and then up a flight of stairs.

At the top of these Nicholas paused. "Is she now?" he said. "So that's what they look like nowadays, the female dons." He surveyed Paula with interest. "She'll make a good role model for you, Biddy. What the's matter, child? Have I said something wrong? I thought you youngsters had to have role models nowadays. They hadn't invented them when I was young, so we had to grow up our own way. What would you like for breakfast, Madam Professor Paula? Bacon and eggs? Or muesli and orange juice? We've got both. Come into the kitchen and choose."

He moved towards the door, but Paula lingered a moment to speak to Bridget, who was looking embarrassed and rather desperate.

"I like your grandpa, I do truly," she whispered. "I think

you're very lucky to have him. And he's lucky to have you."

"Your eggs, Paula," came a loud voice from the kitchen. "How do you like them? Sunny-side up?"

The breakfast was excellent, and Nicholas would not allow any sustained conversation until it was eaten. Then he said, "Now what's going on, Biddy? Don't think I didn't hear that three A.M. phone call and your rushing out of the house. I suppose it's that boy with the saintly name again."

"His mother's dead." Bridget quickly explained. "He swears he didn't hit her."

"But you don't believe him?"

"They're always quarreling," said Bridget unhappily.

"So where do you think he's gone?"

"I thought he might come here."

"Well he didn't. Where else?"

"Maybe somebody else in the group. May. Or Tom. They live nearest."

"Would he trust them?"

"No, probably not," said Bridget reluctantly. "I can't think of anything else. Unless he's gone to Dr. Broadbent's surgery."

"We can soon find that out. I'll call her."

Paula had been listening with interest and some impatience to this exchange, and when Nicholas left the room to telephone she immediately asked Bridget what the group was about.

"James and I thought it was some sort of cover-up," she added. "Not necessarily anything sinister. A roundabout way to get Zavvy's mother off the booze, for example."

"Why should you think that?" Bridget sounded offended. "Didn't Mr. or Mrs. Macgregor explain? We're trying to bridge the generation gap. That's why Grandpa comes along."

"Oh." Paula was surprised and felt herself rebuked. "I'm

sorry," she went on. "It's the fault of the academic mind, not to accept the obvious but always to look for subtleties and complications. Though in all fairness to James and myself, I think if we had heard about it from you or your grandfather we wouldn't have been suspicious. But it was the way Zavvy's mother was talking, and the fact that James's old aunt and uncle are both rich and vulnerable—"

"Yes, I know," broke in Bridget. "I know how you felt. But we really are trying to get old people and young people together. We have some interesting discussions and we do some good work. Gardening and house painting for pensioners, the usual things."

Paula asked more questions. The answers were reassuring, but somehow she felt cheated. James would feel the same, she knew, and in his present state of mind he would blame her, Paula, for suggesting that there could be a sinister background to the events at his aunt's house, and not just a sordid little quarrel between an unstable alcoholic mother and an equally unstable son.

Nicholas Wild came back into the living room. "He's not at the doctor's surgery," he said, and with a quick change of voice, added, "What's the matter? Have you two been quarreling?"

Paula, who up till now had been enjoying the old man's peculiarities, was taken aback by the abruptness of the question, and was even more displeased by Bridget's response.

"They thought there was something sinister about our meetings, Grandpa," she said. "Paula and James."

"Sinister?"

The old man turned to Paula, raising his eyebrows and opening his eyes wide. For the first time she noticed that they were very blue, surprisingly so for his age, and their expression was not very friendly.

"Sinister is much too strong a word," said Paula.

What is the matter with me this morning, she was angrily asking herself. First of all she had let the boy get away, and then she had let herself be taken in by the easy friendliness of these complete strangers into saying something indiscreet. She knew nothing whatever about them; they might be telling the truth and they might not. How could she retrieve her error without making things worse? Certainly not by emphasizing how vulnerable James's old aunt and uncle were. Put the blame on Verena, that would be best.

"It was the way Xavier's mother was describing it," she said aloud. "James and I both dislike sociological jargon, and from what you said a little earlier about role models, Mr. Wild, I suspect that you do too. That's what started me making silly remarks about the generation gap group."

She stopped abruptly. Her instinct was to continue with her explanation, but she remembered that it was fatal to protest too much.

Nicholas appeared to be satisfied. His face recovered its geniality and he damned the sociological jargon as heartily as Paula could wish. Bridget protested that sociologists were only using their own technical terms; other experts had their technical language—economists, physicists, botanists, even artists—you name it—and nobody complained that they were talking jargon.

"That's because they are genuine subjects of study," retorted her grandfather, "and not just glorified gossip, which is what most social surveys consist of. 'When did you last visit a brothel?'—'When did you last commit adultery?'—Gossip. That's all it is. Isn't it, Paula?"

Paula gave her qualified agreement, and the little discussion that ensued seemed on the surface to be as friendly and relaxed as before, but Paula no longer felt at ease. She had caught a glimpse of some very different sorts of feelings—at least on the part of the old man. Whether or not they were shared by Bridget she could not tell. Perhaps she could find out. They knew she was curious about the group; to ask further questions surely couldn't make things any worse.

"Do other older people come to the meetings?" she said, turning to Bridget.

"Well, there's Zavvy's mother," began the girl.

Paula laughed. "That counts as old! Then I must be included too."

"Oh Paula! I'm sorry."

"You're forgiven. Actually I'd rather like to come to a meeting if visitors are allowed. But maybe you won't be going on with it, now that Zavvy's mother is dead and Zavvy has disappeared."

She waited for a response, but neither of the others reacted. Nicholas seemed to have withdrawn into his own thoughts and Bridget was obviously finding it a strain to keep up the conversation.

Paula got to her feet. "I'd better go. We've all got things to attend to. Many thanks for the hospitality—it's ages since I had such a wonderful breakfast."

She knew that she sounded gushing, almost inane, but she no longer cared. There was no more to be learned here at the moment. This odd little household, that she had at first found so appealing, had turned sour on her, and all because of an unguarded look on an old man's face.

Sinister, that was the word that had started it off. As she walked to the bus stop, Paula was mentally telling James all about it. Her irritation with him had almost completely disappeared. She would go home to Hampstead now, because somebody must see to the cats and the mail and the answer-phone, but she would certainly return to James's relatives as soon as she possibly could.

6

The phone was ringing when Paula at last reached home.

"Where on earth have you been?" demanded James, when she rushed to pick up the receiver. "I've been calling for ages."

"Tell you later. What's happening?"

"Xavier's been arrested." James sounded slightly calmer. "He turned up at the police station and told them he'd killed his mother."

"Did they believe him?"

"Not entirely. Apparently he was very high on whatever it is he's hooked on. Dr. Broadbent has been to see him and she and Uncle Mac have fixed for his release on condition he stays in the detoxification clinic that she works for."

"I'm glad about that. I don't think that boy's to blame, James. It's just a hunch."

"That's odd. Uncle Mac thinks the boy's innocent. It seemed to me obvious . . . but anyway, the inspector wants to speak to you some time. I gave him our phone number, but—"

"Perhaps I'd better come back to your aunt's," suggested Paula.

"It's an awful bore for you," he said rather stiffly.

Paula interpreted this to mean that their unspoken misunderstanding was now at an end and that he badly wanted her to return to his relatives' home.

"I'll have to attend to everything here," she said. "I'll probably be at least a couple of hours. How is Aunt Isobel?"

"Not too good. She's asking for you. She seems to have taken a fancy to you."

"The feeling is mutual," said Paula, feeling extraordinarily gratified. "Have you managed to find anybody to take Verena's place?"

"That's the trouble. Aunt Isobel has taken a violent dislike to him."

"Him? Why not a woman?"

"He's an ex-army man with a lot of nursing experience, and he's willing to do housework as well. The agency highly recommended him. Uncle Mac thought it a good idea."

"Well, if *he* thinks so—"

"He isn't infallible." James sounded snappy again, from which Paula deduced that there was tension developing between him and the old man.

"What do you think of the agency man?" she asked.

"Nobody here cares what I think. Of all the obstinate old— Sorry, Paula."

"I'll be as quick as I can," she soothed him. "Give my love to Aunt Isobel. There's the front doorbell. Goodbye for now."

The caller turned out to be a neighbor wanting to talk, and this was followed by several telephone calls. By the time Paula finally got away, the afternoon was well advanced, and the traffic buildup caused further delay to her return to Barley Avenue.

James came running out of the house to greet her.

"I thought you were never coming."

Paula began to explain as they headed into the house. He

interrupted her. "Aunt Isobel's asking for you. She's practically hysterical. She won't talk to anybody else and she won't let Kevin Casey come into her room."

"Kevin—?"

"The guy from the agency. She starts screaming if he comes near her. I just don't know what to do." James paused at the foot of the stairs. "I wasn't keen on his coming, but I must admit that he's quiet and efficient and even quite a good cook. We had an excellent lunch. He's cleaned up the summer house and done other jobs without waiting to be asked. Verena doesn't seem to have been very conscientious."

"But Aunt Isobel liked her," muttered Paula. "Or at least she seemed to like having her here. I'd better go up now, James."

He made room for her to pass.

"Would you like some tea?" he called after her.

"Yes please."

"Then I'll get it sent up."

Aunt Isobel's room was large and rather austere. The general impression was of dark mahogany furniture and heavy green drapes. At first Paula could see no sign of the old lady, and then she heard her voice, unexpectedly firm, coming from the direction of the bay window.

"Come here, my dear. I'm not supposed to stand up."

Paula ran towards the winged armchair.

"Sit down," commanded Aunt Isobel, pointing towards a low stool a couple of feet away, "and let me look at you."

Paula obeyed.

"Yes, James made a good choice, though I doubt if he deserves you."

The voice was still steady, but Paula had the impression that Aunt Isobel was controlling herself with difficulty. She looked more frail than ever, a tiny little figure in a dark blue dressing gown, slumped down low in the great armchair.

Paula was about to make some tactful reply when there came a knock at the door, and Aunt Isobel's control began to slip.

"I expect that's my tea," said Paula, "but I won't let anybody in, I promise you."

As she got up, she reached out to touch the old lady's hand. Both hands grasped at hers. They were very dry, very cold, but they had surprising strength in them.

"I must go," said Paula, "and stop them from coming in."

"Yes, that's right. You do that."

Paula's hand was released.

The bedroom door was actually being opened as she approached it. A short, sandy-haired man of indeterminate age stood there, holding a small tray.

"Your tea, Professor," he said in an expressionless voice. "Dr. Goff asked me to bring it. Where would you like me to put the tray?"

"I'll take it," said Paula. "Thank you for your trouble."

"No trouble, madam."

Neatly he sidestepped her movement to take the tray. "I'll leave it here." He set it down on the bedside table, then looked towards the window.

Paula looked too, and for a moment she thought that Aunt Isobel had somehow managed to disappear. Then she realized the old lady must be crouching down so low in the big armchair that from where they stood, she was not visible.

Why was she so afraid of this man? Paula was determined not to leave this room until she had found out. Meanwhile a silent battle of wills seemed to be developing between herself and the newcomer. Kevin Casey made no move to leave, although there was no reason for him to stay any longer. Paula stepped between him and the window.

"Thank you," she said, when it became obvious that he was not going to speak. "I don't think we need anything else at the moment."

"The bell is here, by the bed," he said. "If you have any trouble with her, let me know at once."

With a final glance towards the window, and a slight inclination of the head, he left the room at last.

Paula hastily poured herself some tea and wondered for a crazy moment whether it was safe to drink it, so strong had been the impression of menace produced by the agency nurse. Then she instantly scolded herself and drank.

Aunt Isobel peered round the side of her chair. "Has he gone?"

"Yes." Paula refilled her cup and resumed her former seat opposite the old lady. "Would you like to tell me about it?" she asked gently. "You know this man, don't you? You've met him before."

Aunt Isobel did not reply, but her features seemed to become convulsed and she made little gasping sounds. Instinctively Paula looked round for the little bottle containing the white tablets, before she realized that the old lady was not having a heart attack, but was shedding tears.

Paula looked away, filled with a mixture of pity and revulsion. Weeping is for the young, she thought; one doesn't expect old people to have the strength for such indulgence, nor does one expect them to have the emotions that would warrant it.

She got up, took the teacup that she had used and carried it over to the washbasin, rinsed it, poured out more tea, and offered it to Aunt Isobel. The old woman had quickly recovered and took it with a faint smile and said, "The English remedy for every ill is tea. In Scotland it is whisky."

"Would you like some?" asked Paula.

"No, no. Tea will do. Don't let's waste any more time. That man. Of course I know him. I met him a year or two ago when I was in prison. He was one of the wardens."

"In prison," repeated Paula, wondering whether Aunt Isobel's mind was wandering, although in fact she had spoken with strength and in a very rational manner and was continuing in similar tones.

"They called it a clinic. For drunkards and nerve cases. I was a nerve case."

"You were ill? Did James know about it?"

"James never knew. I believe he was in America at the time. I had a sort of breakdown. It didn't last very long, but my husband and I felt I could not be properly looked after at home. I believe I was wandering about the road in my nightgown."

The old lady suddenly gave a little snort of laughter. "I am told that is not uncommon," she added, "among the aged and the senile."

"I believe not," agreed Paula.

"I don't know what caused it. I'd had the first heart attack and perhaps wasn't fully recovered. Anyway, I've never done it again, although perhaps I am a little forgetful now and then."

"So am I," murmured Paula. "So are all of us, of whatever age or condition of life."

"Yes." The old lady sighed and shut her eyes. The effort of speaking seemed temporarily to have exhausted her, and Paula waited with as much patience as she could muster.

"The clinic was a very superior place," went on Aunt Isobel at last. "Not very far from here. I believe they have sent that poor wretched boy there. The one with the outlandish papist name."

"Xavier?"

"Yes. Of all the absurdities! Why couldn't they call him Robert or William? I am sorry, my dear." She stretched out a hand to touch Paula's knee. "I am digressing. Please forgive me. I have never spoken of this. Not even to my husband. But I must speak now. Just let me take my time."

"Perhaps you'd like some more tea? Or whisky?"

"No, no. I'm quite all right. Just assembling my thoughts. That man—Casey—was a nurse at the clinic. I believe he was second-in-command. The matron was a very superior individual whom one hardly ever saw. Casey was the one who did the work. And the other resident nurse—whom you know already—"

"Not Verena!" Paula could not help exclaiming.

"Mrs. Keeling. The 'Mrs.' is a courtesy title. Some of these women are strangely old-fashioned when it comes to admitting they have no husband. Yes, Verena, as we will call her—what a name!—looked after me in the clinic. Perfectly adequately, I must admit, as far as my physical comforts were concerned. She was not a qualified nurse, of course, but she was a good cook and not a bad housekeeper. Otherwise I would never have been able to persuade my husband to have her here."

A suspicion began to form in Paula's mind. The Verena situation was at last beginning to make some sense.

"She applied to you for the job?" she asked.

"We put an advertisement in the local paper," was the reply, "as well as informing the employment agencies. Verena wrote, reminding me of my time in the clinic, and also reminding me of certain matters that—"

Aunt Isobel broke off suddenly and there followed a long pause, during which she turned her head and stared out of the window.

The suspicion that had arisen in Paula's mind began to take firmer shape. Some sort of blackmail, she said to herself. Whatever could it be? Was Aunt Isobel's stay in this clinic to be kept a secret? And had Verena threatened to make it public if she wasn't given the job?

Paula thought this was not impossible. James had not known about the breakdown, and Aunt Isobel was only talking now because she was so afraid.

"Aunt Isobel," she said gently, when it seemed as if the silence was never going to end. "May I ask you something?"

The old lady inclined her head slightly, still keeping her face averted.

"All this business about a group who meet to try and bridge the gap between the generations—is there any truth in that at all?"

"There's some truth," replied Aunt Isobel. "I'm sorry, Paula, that I felt obliged to talk a lot of nonsense, though I think Verena really believed it all. She was always babbling about the local Youth Club. The boy used to go there and she was worried about him. Drugs, I believe. She asked if the group could meet here, but I've no doubt that somebody else put her up to it."

Paula's thoughts went first to Kevin Casey and then to the breakfast with Bridget and her grandfather, Nicholas Wild. Aunt Isobel must surely know of him as a member of the group. Was there any link-up between him and the people at the clinic? And in any case, why had these two, Kevin and Verena, left the staff of the clinic?

She was bursting with questions. Aunt Isobel would not know the answers to all of them, but she plainly knew some. Unfortunately she seemed to have come to the end of her strength. Her eyes were closed and she looked completely drained.

After a few minutes' silence she seemed to become aware of Paula's scrutiny and of the thoughts that lay behind it.

"Yes, I was being blackmailed," she said, obviously

speaking only with a great effort. "I can't tell you more now. Help me, Paula. Stay with me."

She stretched out a hand for Paula to hold. It was clearly pointless to try to press her further, but there was one question that Paula felt she had to ask.

"What about your husband," she said. "Can't he do anything for you? Does he know about this?"

"My husband looks after my medicines and our finances," was the uncompromising reply. "Apart from that we rarely communicate, and you will kindly not mention anything of this conversation to him."

Paula gave her promise.

"Stay in this house. Don't let that man come near me."

"I'll do my best," said Paula.

"And don't tell anybody what I've told you. Not even James."

"I'm sorry," said Paula, "but I really can't promise that. I've no standing in this household. I'm only here because of James. I can't possibly do what you ask unless I tell him at least something of what you have told me."

"Than make it as little as you possibly can. Men! There's things they don't understand and never will."

7

Talking to James turned out to be far from easy, not because of any reluctance on either side, but because of the difficulty of finding privacy. They had only just settled in the big sitting room, when Kevin Casey came in to apologize for disturbing them, and to add that he was only going to rearrange some ornaments that he had misplaced earlier in the day.

"That's all right," said James, getting up. "We were just about to go into the garden."

But the garden proved no refuge, because within two minutes of their moving the chairs into the remaining sunlight on the lawn, Kevin suddenly appeared again.

"Excuse me, sir," he said in his best deferential manner to James, "but I am just about to prepare the evening meal. Would soup followed by cold meat and salad be in order?"

"If Mr. Macgregor thinks," began James.

"Mr. Macgregor is resting," interposed Kevin smoothly. "He particularly asked not to be disturbed. Mrs. Macgregor appears to have locked her door. Very unwise, if you will forgive my saying so, in her state of health. Should she suffer an attack, there will be considerable difficulty in coming to her assistance."

"I'll speak to her about it," said James in unnaturally subdued tones.

Whatever is it about this man, wondered Paula, that makes us all so nervous of him? He's like a malevolent Jeeves.

"Thank you, sir," said Kevin, and proceeded to perform his little bow of sneering respect before departing.

James and Paula looked at each other, and then both spoke at once: "The summer house."

"At least we'll be able to see him coming," added Paula.

But when they got there they found the sliding glass doors would not shift.

James swore. "Kevin must have given the key to Uncle Mac after he cleaned up here."

"Or kept it himself. We'll just have to walk up and down at this end of the lawn."

"He'll see us, he'll be laughing at us," muttered James.

"That can't be helped. Are you listening?"

Hastily Paula told him that Verena and Kevin seemed to have some sort of hold over Aunt Isobel. Respecting the old lady's wishes, she did not mention the time in the clinic, but went on to describe her breakfast with Bridget and her grandfather.

"It looks as if Verena really believed in the geronto-phobes," said James thoughtfully. "But you don't think the old man did?"

"I'm sure he didn't."

"An artist. Is he forging pictures?"

"I think it's quite possible. I'm sure the shop is just a cover. But I don't think that's relevant in this case. Your folks here haven't any pictures worth stealing."

"Oh, I don't know." James sounded a trifle offended. "Some of those Victorian prints—"

"Very minor," interrupted Paula. "Not important enough

to get Verena planted here so that they could carry out—carry out what, James? Supposing Kevin Casey and Nicholas Wild are conspiring together to rob your uncle and aunt. They want to have the run of this house. What are they after?"

"You've seen the house," replied James, still sounding a little aloof. "There's plenty of good solid furniture and ornaments, but nothing important enough, as you put it, to warrant such a complicated and risky scheme as planting a housekeeper here and keeping an eye on her activities via this bogus group therapy business."

"All the same," said Paula, turning briskly to walk back across the lawn, "it makes sense if they really do want to get into the house for some purpose of their own, and if Verena found out what it was all about and didn't like it—well, she's dead now. An accident, with luck, and if not, then that crazy son of hers will be suspected."

James had to admit that this was a very plausible hypothesis.

"So you think that Kevin isn't just nasty, but actually crooked? Possibly even a murderer?"

"Yes, I do," said Paula emphatically, convincing herself more and more even as she spoke. "And if Aunt Isobel knows something about him, and he knows she does, then she has every reason to be very frightened."

James groaned. "My fault, I suppose. But I don't think I could have stopped Uncle Mac taking him on. He's an obstinate old sod."

"Uncle Mac," repeated Paula thoughtfully. "Did I tell you what Aunt Isobel said about him? 'My husband looks after my medicines and our finances, but otherwise we hardly communicate.' "

"Good Lord, did she really say that? Less than twenty-four hours since you first met her, Paula, and you've learned more about them than I have in twice that number of years!"

"Families," sighed Paula. "They never really know each other. They only hate or love each other. What do *you* think Aunt Isobel meant? Surely not that she doesn't trust Uncle Mac?"

"She's the one who's got the money," said James grimly, "and he's ten years younger than she is. My grandfather left everything to Isobel—his only sister and last surviving relative. Except myself, of course, but you'll remember that I was still very much persona non grata when he died."

Paula did indeed remember. The fire that consumed the family home and all its contents shortly after the death of James's famous novelist grandfather had been very much a turning point in the lives of both James and herself, although they had not realized this at the time.

"So if Aunt Isobel dies—" she began.

"Uncle Mac presumably gets the lot. But for heaven's sake, Paula—"

"You've just said he's much younger than she is. He could reasonably look forward to ten years or more of free and prosperous widowerhood."

"And he looks after her medicines. Oh, this is absurd!" exclaimed James, suddenly standing still in the middle of the lawn. "If Uncle Mac wanted to get rid of her he could easily do it at any time without anybody suspecting."

"Very true. I think we'd better go in. I can see Kevin the Menace advancing on us again. And I'm awfully hungry."

Uncle Mac was already seated at the end of the dining room table and did not look too pleased at being kept waiting for his soup. He ignored Paula and addressed himself to James.

"Where's your aunt? I thought you'd gone to fetch her."

"I'll go and see if she wants to come down," said James, obviously controlling his annoyance with some difficulty.

Paula put a hand on his arm. "I'll go," she murmured.

"That would be best," he said, smiling at her. "Thanks."

Paula quickly left the room. She had the impression that an argument was about to develop, and that Kevin, now entering with a tray, would relish it and encourage it. In fact it looked like it would be a most uncomfortable meal. Whether it would be made worse or better by Aunt Isobel's presence she could not begin to guess, but she felt fairly confident that the old lady would not want to come down. She was surprised therefore to find Aunt Isobel dressed and apparently determined on joining them.

"Kevin will be sure he's frightened me away," she said, "and I want to spoil his triumph."

Paula made a little gesture of applause. "I'll back you up," she said, holding out an arm for Aunt Isobel's support.

It was thus that they entered the dining room, Aunt Isobel making the most of her five-foot-one-inch size and looking defiantly around as she took her seat at the end of the table, opposite Uncle Mac. Paula remained at her left, several feet away, since the table was large and long, and James sat across from her at a similar distance from his uncle and aunt.

For at least half a minute there was complete silence. James sat frowning at his place setting. Uncle Mac stared into space, and Paula glanced at Kevin. He stood perfectly still behind Uncle Mac's chair, the perfect servant, but Paula thought she could detect a mixture of annoyance and malevolence in his expression.

Aunt Isobel was the first to speak. "Well, Mr. Casey," she said, and the trembling of her voice was barely noticeable, "now that we are all assembled, we should like to proceed with our dinner."

"Certainly, madam."

It was said with all the contempt of which he was capable.

For a moment Paula feared that Aunt Isobel was either going to make some sharp retort or burst into tears. Fortunately James awoke from his brooding and snapped at Kevin.

"Hurry up, then. What are we waiting for?"

Kevin disappeared at once. Uncle Mac looked disapprovingly at James. Paula, turning to comfort Aunt Isobel, saw the old lady looking perfectly composed and very pleased with herself. The change from her former state of apprehension was remarkable. Paula was relieved, but at the same time worried. If Kevin Casey really was threatening her in some way, this method of provoking him was not going to lessen the threat. She was beginning to think that she had better stay with Aunt Isobel all the time, day and night.

Just then the soup arrived. It was a tomato soup that had obviously come from a can or a packet, and Paula, hungry and tired and grateful for any refreshment, took up her spoon. Aunt Isobel did likewise, took a sip of the liquid, put the spoon down on the plate, wiped her mouth with her napkin, and said in a firm clear voice, "This soup is most unpalatable. But then what can one expect from a slovenly nurse who got the sack for blackmailing his patients."

There was an audible gasp from the three others seated at the table. Then all eyes turned towards the door. It was open, but Kevin had not yet left the room. Holding the empty tray in front of him like a shield, he walked slowly towards Uncle Mac, stopped still, and said, "May I make a suggestion, Mr. Macgregor?"

"Yes, yes, go on," said the old man impatiently.

"I quite appreciate," went on Kevin very deliberately, "that I am here in a domestic and not a custodial capacity, but I feel it my duty, sir, to give you a word of warning."

He paused. Uncle Mac gave a grunt and attacked his

soup. Paula glanced at Aunt Isobel and noticed that she was now doing the same.

Kevin continued, "In my humble opinion, sir, Mrs. Macgregor is showing all the symptoms that led previously to her unfortunate—er—lapses—that were the reason for her being entrusted to our care. These conditions are liable to recur with advancing years. My advice would be to consult a specialist before the condition deteriorates any further. Thank you for listening to me."

He made a little bow, turned, and left the room. He had not once looked at Aunt Isobel, neither had Uncle Mac once looked at her, during this exchange.

Paula and James stared at each other across the table, silently communicating bewilderment and helplessness. The two old people continued to drink the despised soup with every appearance of satisfaction. Surely, thought Paula, they can't just be going to ignore this completely. The silence became oppressive. Paula began to feel slightly hysterical. She looked appealingly at James and was relieved when he responded with a slight nod of the head before turning to his uncle.

"What's all this about? When was Auntie in the hospital? Why didn't anybody tell me?"

"There wasn't any need," said the old man. "You were in America. She wasn't ill for very long."

"But what was the matter?" persisted James. "I do think I ought to have been told."

"You couldn't have done anything. It was all over by the time you got home."

James gave a little grunt of impatience and turned to his aunt. Paula looked at her too. The old woman had finished her soup and was sitting with her hands clasped and resting on the table. She was looking straight ahead at her husband, but Paula could see the expression on her face quite clearly, and found it alarming. There was triumph in it, which was hardly surprising, but also a sort of wildness that Paula had not noticed in Aunt Isobel before. There had been some forgetfulness and confusion, even some agitation, when Paula and James had first arrived and been told about Verena's generation-gap group, but Paula had seen no signs of mental disturbance. Nor had it occurred to her, while listening to Aunt Isobel fearfully relating the story of her breakdown, to doubt that the old lady had made a complete recovery, and that any appearance of mental disorder was simply the result of the dilemma in which she found herself with the arrival of Kevin Casey.

Now, however, Paula found herself beginning to wonder. At first she had been glad that Aunt Isobel seemed to have conquered her fears, but the change from apprehension to aggressiveness, in fact vindictiveness, was unnatural, hardly credible except as the result of some imbalance.

Could she believe anything that Aunt Isobel had been telling her? The thought was very disagreeable but it could not be put aside. She looked across the table at James, seeking comfort, but there was none to be found. He had pushed aside his soup, untouched, and was staring first at one, then at the other of his elderly relatives, almost as if he was seeing them for the first time. He's exasperated, thought Paula, but he's also terribly worried. He's thinking just what I am thinking: is Aunt Isobel really going out of her mind, and if so, what are we going to do about it?

Meanwhile the subject of their concern was finishing the despised soup with every appearance of enjoyment. She put down her spoon, wiped her mouth with her napkin, looked around, and said, "What's next, I wonder? I rather fancy a nice bit of finnan haddock but I don't suppose we'll be having that."

It sounded very normal, very sane, an innocent example

of an old person's interest in food. Uncle Mac said he rather fancied it too, but that he was afraid there would only be cold meat and salad.

"Do you remember," said Aunt Isobel, "that little hotel where we stayed in Aberdeen?"

"Never forgotten it," said her husband. "They knew how to cook fish."

The reminiscences continued for some time, in perfect amity, and with the Scottishness becoming more marked every moment. The presence of Kevin Casey in the house, indeed of Paula and James as well, seemed to have been completely forgotten by the old couple. Is this how they behave when they are alone, wondered Paula, or is Uncle Mac putting on an act, trying to soothe her? Or are they both acting for our benefit?

James, obviously relieved that the conversation had taken so harmless a direction, began to join in too, and even the arrival of Kevin with the expected dishes did not disturb the harmony. It was as if the unpleasant start to the meal had never been.

Finally Aunt Isobel got up from her chair and addressed Kevin with great dignity.

"We will have our coffee in the drawing room, Mrs. Goff and I. No doubt the gentlemen will join us later."

Paula had the sense of having walked into a Victorian novel. A smile and a gesture of resignation from James brought her back to reality. They do behave like this sometimes, she told herself. This is quite normal and he wants me to go along with it. She got up and held out an arm to Aunt Isobel, who took it in a queenly manner.

As they left the room Paula turned to look at Kevin. He was standing behind Uncle Mac's chair, absolutely motionless except for his eyes. They were very pale blue and they turned upon Paula and James's aunt. The hatred in them was unmistakable. It completely shook Paula out of her fantasy of the Victorian household and she firmly resolved that whatever Aunt Isobel said or did, she must not be left alone this coming night.

8

In the drawing room, alone with Paula, Aunt Isobel had a short period of weakness. Sunk back in a chair, eyes closed, face pale except for two hectic red spots on her cheeks, she looked every minute of her ninety-plus years.

Paula took her hand. Aunt Isobel responded feebly.

After a few minutes of great anxiety, Paula heard her give a little cough and begin to speak.

"Did I put on a good act at dinner?"

"You certainly made an impression," replied Paula cautiously.

"On *him*, do you mean?"

"On Kevin Casey. He looked very annoyed."

Aunt Isobel smiled faintly but said nothing. Paula began to feel irritated with her. "Was it wise to treat him like that, if you really are afraid that—"

"I'm not afraid," interrupted Aunt Isobel. "Not any longer, now that I've decided what I'm going to do with it, and now that I've got you to help me."

"How can I help you? And to do with what? I haven't the least idea what you are talking about."

Paula spoke quite sharply. She was beginning to have the sense of being manipulated. Had all that fearfulness before dinner been an act as well? And had all her own sympathy and protectiveness been deliberately aroused and played upon? These were most uncomfortable thoughts. She would almost prefer to think Aunt Isobel mentally unbalanced than to think of her as scheming and manipulative. But maybe she was both. That would explain a lot.

"I'll tell you later, when you come to my room," said Aunt Isobel. "Somebody's coming."

The "somebody" was James with a coffee tray, followed by Uncle Mac.

"Casey is in a huff," said the latter. "You shouldn't have teased him like that, Bella."

"He shouldn't have said I was going out of my mind," she retorted.

"He didn't. Not till after you'd been so offensive to him."

"I wouldn't have needed to if you had protected me. But you never do stand up for me. I need never have gone into that clinic if you'd helped me to get better at home. But you just couldn't wait to put me away. That's all you want, isn't it, Macgregor? You'd like me to be shut up in a lunatic asylum and declared incapable so that you can get your hands on my money."

Uncle Mac began to protest, but his wife, speaking loudly and firmly, ignored him and went on, "But I've news for you, Macgregor, and you won't like it one little bit. There isn't any money. Not anymore. That imbecile financial adviser whom you made me listen to has embezzled the lot. There isn't any money so there's no point in putting me away. So you and your Mr. Casey can give up your schemes, and you can send him away immediately. Tonight. Do you hear me?"

Her voice rose to a scream. The red spots on her cheeks stood out more vividly than ever.

Uncle Mac put a hand on her wrist. "Careful, Bella.

You'll have another attack. Please try to calm yourself. I had no idea who this man Casey was. I never saw him when I visited you at the clinic. He was highly recommended by the agency. If I had known—"

"You knew, you knew!" screamed the old woman.

James and Paula had been standing a few feet away from the old couple, too astonished to intervene. Now they came forward. James leaned down and put an arm round his aunt. "Please, Auntie," he begged, "don't go on like this. Uncle Mac didn't know anything about Casey, neither did I. We're neither of us to blame, and if he upsets you so much we'll tell him to go tomorrow and get somebody else in to look after you."

"Tomorrow! Why not tonight?"

"Well, it's rather awkward," began James.

"Awkward my foot! The man's a thief. He might even be a murderer."

There was a moment's silence and then Uncle Mac spoke to his wife in a voice that Paula had not heard from him before.

"Be careful, Bella. That's a very grave accusation, and you know what it could lead to."

It was quiet but very menacing and there was not the least trace of affection in it.

Aunt Isobel made no reply, but she shrank back in her chair and looked very like the frightened old woman whom Paula had tried to comfort only a few hours ago.

"I do think you'd better be careful, Auntie," said James in much kinder tones. "We've promised to get rid of the fellow tomorrow, and meanwhile the less said about it the better."

"You stupid boy," said Aunt Isobel, rallying slightly. "You don't know anything about it."

"Then isn't it high time I was told!" snapped James, suddenly losing his temper, which was a rare occurrence with him. "You call me late in the evening at great inconvenience to Paula and myself and when we get here you spin us some idiotic story about your new housekeeper and her generation-gap group and then she gets herself murdered—if it *was* murder, which I seriously doubt—but you say nothing at all about the fact that you were quite recently in a psychiatric clinic and that she was an assistant there, and then—"

"Who told you that? I never told you." Aunt Isobel came fully to life again. "I told Paula. I told her not to tell anyone."

"Paula didn't tell me," James almost shouted. "Mac's just told me. I made him tell me. And I'm really annoyed—in fact I'm really distressed—that neither of you told me you were in the clinic. How on earth can I be expected to help you if you keep something like that secret from me?"

His aunt made no reply. She was clutching her chest and gasping for breath. Her husband produced the little bottle with the white tablets.

"Get her to bed," he muttered. "No point in talking any more now. She always has an attack if she doesn't want to answer a question."

James and Paula stood back slightly while the scene of the previous evening was repeated. Uncle Mac tended his wife with great gentleness and care. It would have been reassuring, even rather moving, if there had not been that earlier revelation of a very different side to him.

As soon as they were out of the room James mentioned this. "I've never known him to speak to her like that before. They've always seem such a devoted couple."

The phrase irritated Paula. It occurred to her that James was getting rather a habit of speaking in clichés. Or perhaps he had always done so but she had never noticed it until they actually made a home together. All her misgivings returned in full force. She never ought to have got involved with his relations, never, never. But she was deep into it now and she would never rest until she knew what was really going on in this household.

"Devoted couple," she repeated, unable to keep a note of bitterness out of her voice. "Does such a thing exist? Isn't it just that people get used to each other and would miss the irritations, just as one gets used to having a hole in a tooth?"

She regretted her words even as she was speaking them, but James was obviously too worried to want to argue.

"I don't like this clinic business one little bit. What do you think, Paula? Is she mentally unbalanced?"

"A few hours ago I'd have said certainly not," replied Paula, "but after this evening I don't feel quite so sure. Her behavior to Kevin . . . did Uncle Mac explain that he was working in the clinic too?"

James swore fervently. "Okay," he said at last, controlling himself. "Tell me about it."

Paula did so, then added, "You know, James, I think she has very good reason to be scared, and that makes her seem a little mad. She's terrified of Kevin, and she was scared of Verena, but not, I think, of Xavier. It may well be that she is also scared of Uncle Mac, but being so very dependent on him . . ."

There was no need to finish the sentence. James was moving restlessly about the room, muttering, "I wish I'd known. If only someone had told me—"

"That's odd in itself," interrupted Paula. "They're always asking your help on trivial matters, but when it's something really important . . . Let's assume somebody wanted her out of the house for a while and chose the weeks when you were in the U.S.A. A faked mental breakdown. Drug-induced? Uncle Mac knows all about that sort of thing. He doesn't want to harm her. If he wanted her dead he could easily fix it. Why should he want her out of the house?"

"Because—because she's got something he wants to get hold of."

"Then why not drug her and take it while she's asleep?"

"He's tried that. He couldn't find it. She's been very clever in her choice of a hiding place."

"The summer house. Hidden in the foundations. Aren't we getting melodramatic?" added Paula with a smile.

"My folks *are* melodramatic," retorted James. "Particularly my famous grandfather's generation. Don't forget she's his sister."

"His sister. Yes indeed. Sister of a very famous novelist. Did he leave her any money, James? Yes, of course. Quite a lot. But it can't be that. As we keep saying, if Uncle Mac really wanted to inherit it before she dies naturally . . . but wait a moment. Supposing she's made a will not leaving it to her husband?"

James shook his head. "No go. It all comes to him. Actually I suspect there isn't so very much left. They've been living on capital."

"And they spend very freely. He must be getting worried, James."

For a little while they sat in silence, drinking coffee and thinking. Then Paula said, "Your grandfather, Aunt Isobel's brother, the illustrious G.E. Goff. Perhaps he didn't only leave her money. Perhaps he bequeathed her something else. Manuscripts, for example. Didn't you talk to her when you were collecting material to help me write my book?"

"Of course I did. She wasn't much help. She shut up like a clam. Didn't want the family's dirty linen washed in public. Incidentally, she very much disapproved of your book."

"But she doesn't seem to disapprove of me."

"I'm not at all sure that she makes the connection." James looked amused. "Sorry, darling, but I'm afraid she regards you merely as an appendage to myself and not as a female scholar of considerable reputation."

"That's a relief," said Paula. She was not referring only to Aunt Isobel, but also to the fact that James sounded much more like his old self, the self she knew and loved. "So what are we going to do," she went on. "If Kevin Casey with or without the connivance of Uncle Mac has insinuated himself into this house with a view to finding and stealing more valuable property of your aunt's, and if he knows he is going to be sent away tomorrow, then tonight will be his last chance."

James put down his coffee cup and started to sing, "Tonight, tonight . . ."

We really have got over a hurdle, thought Paula, we're really together again.

"Come on, let's think," she said aloud.

For several minutes they thought.

"We ought to look at Verena's rooms," said James at last, "since she must have been involved in whatever it is."

"Didn't the police look?"

"Yes, but not with the knowledge of what we now know. Or rather what we think we know," he corrected himself hurriedly.

"Maybe they know more than we think," said Paula. "But I agree that we ought to have a look at the rooms. It's not likely we'll find anything, though, since Kevin has had the run of the house for most of the day and he'll have been up there for sure."

"I'm afraid you're right. The summer house?"

"Verena has had access to the summer house for several weeks," objected Paula.

"But she may not have known what they were looking for."

"If she really was murdered, then she must have known."

"Not necessarily. How about Auntie's room? I'll have to leave that to you, Paula."

"I'll do my best," she said, "but I've a feeling that Uncle Mac is going to keep watch over her tonight, and I may not be able to do . . . Who are you phoning, James?" she interrupted herself.

James had been studying the list of telephone numbers that lay on the coffee table and was about to call a number.

"Dr. Rose Broadbent," he replied. "I want her to come and see Aunt Isobel. Tonight."

"You don't think that she could be in on it too?"

"Well, it's her clinic they put Auntie into, and Xavier's there now."

"You mean she owns the clinic?"

"She's probably got shares in it. Anyway, it's the one she uses for patients."

James spoke into the phone. "That's very good of you, Dr. Broadbent. We don't think she's very bad, but we would be much less worried if you would have a look at her. Many thanks."

He replaced the receiver and pulled a face. "This is where the money goes. She charges hefty fees."

"She did seem to be on very close terms with Uncle Mac," said Paula thoughtfully, "but I hope she's not involved. I rather liked her."

After a little discussion they decided that Paula should go and inspect Verena's rooms while James talked to Dr. Broadbent.

"I think it would be best if you keep out of the way," he added.

Paula was obliged to agree, although she would very much have liked to stay and listen.

9

Paula waited in the bedroom until she could no longer hear the sound of voices coming from the landing. They had all gone into Aunt Isobel's room: James, Uncle Mac, and the doctor. If Aunt Isobel really was ill, thought Paula, then such an invasion would hardly be conducive to her recovery, even if the three of them remained calm and considerate. Judging from the loudness of the voices this was certainly not the case. Dr. Broadbent, behind the professional briskness, was clearly not pleased. Uncle Mac was telling James not to interfere, and James, yet again, was insisting that if he was to be summoned to help, then he had got to be told what was going on.

The door of Aunt Isobel's room closed behind them. Paula went quickly downstairs to check that Kevin was still in the kitchen. There was nobody there, and for a moment she feared that he had guessed her intention and gone ahead of her to the housekeeper's rooms. Or to the room allotted to him, which was on the same floor. Then she looked out of the window and caught a glimpse of him crossing the lawn. The long summer evening was at last giving way to night and in another few seconds he was almost lost to view.

Paula scarcely hesitated before deciding to follow him.

She could look at the housekeeper's rooms tomorrow, after Kevin had left, but this was his last night in the house, and it was much more important to find out what he was going to do with it.

The path to the left of the lawn was bordered by tall shrubs. Several times she was very conscious of the sound of her own footsteps on the gravel, but the man whom she could now see approaching the summer house gave no sign that he suspected he was being followed.

Only when he actually reached his goal did he look round. Paula, hastily concealing herself behind the branches of a big rhododendron, remained perfectly still. For a full minute nothing happened except that a white cat came across the lawn from the direction of the empty house next door and ran straight towards where Paula was hiding.

Silently Paula prayed that the cat would do nothing that would reveal her own presence.

The cat wound itself round her legs without making any sound and then shot off into the bushes. Paula breathed again and peered between the branches at as much as she could see of the summer house.

Kevin appeared to be still standing on the step, making no move to push open the glass door. He was no longer looking in her direction, but seemed to be facing the adjoining garden from which the cat had apparently come.

The house next door had been on the market for a long time, James had said. That meant that the grounds would be very neglected. What were they hiding, wondered Paula, besides providing a haven for wandering cats and other wildlife.

Feeling less tense, but still very suspicious and also puzzled, Paula observed Kevin as he stood there watching. Why didn't he go into the summer house if he had come here once again to search for something? He had the keys, he still had status in the house, and in any case he was never short of excuses for his actions.

If he suspected he was being watched why did he not come forward and challenge her? It almost looked as if he was waiting for somebody. Am I to eavesdrop again, wondered Paula, as I did early this morning when Xavier and his girlfriend were talking?

For a moment or two her attention wandered. Had it really been only that morning? The day seemed to have been going on forever, so much had happened meanwhile. She was aroused from these thoughts by the feel of the white cat brushing round her legs again before running back across the lawn. Paula watched it disappear into the bushes, and as she looked with eyes now more accustomed to the dimness, she could see the branches on that side of the garden move. The cat, with senses so much more acute than those of a human being, had no doubt been aware of the disturbance before she had.

Somebody was coming out from behind the shrubs at the other side of the lawn. Kevin had moved off the step of the summer house and was walking in that direction.

Paula, tense with excitement, forced herself to make no move. That empty house, she was telling herself. Anybody could walk into the grounds. And there must somewhere be a gap in the privet hedge that divided the garden from Aunt Isobel's. Not particularly security-conscious herself, she was yet shocked by the carelessness of the old couple. They seemed to be oblivious of any risk, and the fact that they were so dependent on casual labour and temporary help only made them the more vulnerable.

Aunt Isobel, for all her force of spirit, was physically very frail, but Uncle Mac seemed to be healthy enough. Surely he could take more precautions for their safety? Unless, unless . . .

Aunt Isobel has the money, said Paula to herself. Presumably she pays the bills. On the other hand, she said that he looks after their finances.

Puzzling over this, wondering yet again what was the true nature of the relationship between the two old people, Paula had for a few moments ceased to watch what was going on before her.

She looked up again to see that a meeting was taking place. Standing beside Kevin, a few steps away from the summer house, was a tallish figure, taller than Kevin, obviously a man, seemingly not young, but by no means inactive. They appeared to be talking, but Paula could hear nothing of what was said. She longed to move closer, but it would be crazy to leave her safe hiding place.

A few minutes passed, during which she continued to peer between the branches. She had the impression that Kevin was in some way subordinate to the newcomer. He seemed to be ill at ease, shifting from one foot to the other, whereas the other man stood perfectly still.

She was on the point of making some reckless move, so great was her frustration, when at last she saw the two men move into the summer house, Kevin unlocking the door and leading the way.

A lamp was switched on and for a brief moment Paula saw the face of the newcomer. Nicholas Wild, eccentric artist grandfather of Bridget, who was the girlfriend of Xavier, Verena's son.

Of course Nicholas was in it, whatever "it" might be. He was probably the key to it all. Presumably the meeting had been arranged for Kevin to report progress. Or the lack of it.

Unless they had a specific reason for visiting the summer house. Such as a hiding place for the precious manuscript, said Paula to herself, and suddenly, unaware of having made any decision, she found herself coming out from her own hiding place and walking towards the end of the garden.

The two men had gone through to the kitchen at the back of the summer house. I've a perfect right to go in, thought Paula, lingering at the entrance. I'm a guest in this house. And Kevin's still got a right to be here, and no doubt, if challenged, he would have an excellent excuse for Nicholas's presence. I would gain nothing by announcing myself, but would only increase their suspicions of me, and could even be walking into danger.

As she lingered outside the glass doors, the memory of finding Verena's unconscious body on the floor returned vividly to her mind.

She turned away. They would be coming out at any moment and her previous hiding place was too far to return to. The bushes adjoining the grounds of the empty house were now her nearest shelter. Paula pushed her way between them and found herself at a gap in the privet hedge.

It was very dark. Only the fact that the London night sky was never completely black made it possible for her to make out the shapes of trees and bushes.

In the neighboring garden it was darker than ever, even more overgrown. Without a light it would be pointless to go further, and besides, she was now feeling very uneasy. Not only did she fear that Nicholas might catch up with her, but the darkness and the trees and the thick bushes were beginning to oppress her badly, and the panic of claustrophobia threatened. She hastily retreated back to the Macgregors' garden. Sheltering under the low branches of a beech tree, Paula rested and recovered her nerves. She was now much nearer to the summer house than she had been in her previous hiding place. With luck she would not be discovered, and she could now hear what the two men were saying.

"But I have to leave tomorrow." Kevin's voice was almost deferential.

"Why? Who says so?"

There was not a hint of the genial eccentric in the old man's response.

"The nephew," replied Kevin.

"He's got no authority here. You were employed by Mr. Macgregor."

"Yes, but—"

"Do I have to remind you," said Nicholas in exasperated tones, "that you have an excellent means of persuading Mr. Macgregor to keep you on?"

Kevin did not immediately reply. Then Uncle Mac *is* involved in it, said Paula to herself; or at any rate in part of it. Helping to get Aunt Isobel put away in the clinic, probably.

"It won't work with the nephew," said Kevin at last.

"Then get rid of the nephew. And that sly little wife of his," added Nicholas Wild in a loud voice.

Sly little wife, repeated Paula to herself. Good God, that's me!

Hastily she put a hand over her mouth. The urge to break out into hysterical laughter could scarcely be controlled.

"But you don't know her," Kevin was saying quite defiantly. "I've been making inquiries. She's quite well known, it seems, for ferreting out things and making a nuisance of herself."

"All the more reason to get rid of her," snapped Nicholas. "But I think you're exaggerating. Bridget brought her round to our place for breakfast this morning, and my impression was that she doesn't want to be mixed up in this business at all. She'd walked out and was going home, and I'm surprised she came back."

Kevin muttered something that Paula could not hear.

"Then forget about the nephew and the wife," snapped Nicholas in response. "Stick to Macgregor. Tell him what you're going to do if he doesn't keep you on here. I don't have to teach you the art of blackmail, do I?"

"Okay, if you say so," said Kevin. "And what next? The summer house seems to be useless and I've no idea where else I can look for it. Have you?"

"Not at the moment." For the first time the old man's voice held signs of doubt. "But it's got to be somewhere. You'll have to work on the old woman again."

"She has a heart attack as soon as I seem to be getting anywhere," protested Kevin.

"Then you'll have to do it more subtly. We don't want her dying before we've found out where she's hidden it. That really would put paid to everything. I'll have to go now. Bridget gets worried if I'm out late at night. I don't want her worried. And I don't want to have to come here unless it's absolutely necessary. All right," he added as Kevin began to protest, "you were quite right in sending for me tonight. You needed some fresh instructions. But I don't want any more calls from you until you've got something positive to report. Goodnight."

The conclusion of this conversation was so abrupt that Paula had only time to creep further under the branches of the beech tree before Nicholas approached.

She then waited for what seemed an eternity before she dared to straighten up and come out onto the lawn. To her great relief there was no sign of Kevin, nor was there any light coming from the summer house. It looked as if she could walk back to the house openly and get James on his own as soon as possible.

But the shocks of the evening were not yet over. No sooner had she taken a few steps on the grass when a tall lean figure suddenly appeared in front of her and hands shot out and grabbed her by the arms.

Panic struck again, far worse than it had before, and Paula screamed loudly. At least she thought she screamed, but afterwards she wondered whether she had in fact made much noise.

Then equally suddenly the hands let her go and a young and rather shaky male voice called out, "Christ! It's the wife. The professor's wife."

"Zavvy!" cried Paula, weak with relief. "What are you doing here? Why aren't you in the clinic?"

The boy groaned. "That madhouse! You can't imagine—"

He broke off and then grabbed hold of her again. "You're not to tell anyone. If you're going to tell anyone—"

"Xavier," said Paula very calmly and firmly, "I solemnly promise that nobody shall hear of your presence through me, not even James, who by the way is not my husband, though we do live together."

"Thanks. Sorry," said the boy, letting her go.

"However," Paula continued in the same steady manner, "you've given me an awful fright and I think I deserve to know what you are planning to do. I don't know about you, but I badly need a drink. Coffee preferably. Not alcohol." She looked longingly towards the summer house. "I suppose they've locked up," she added.

"We can get in round the back," said Xavier. "If you don't mind climbing through a window. I'll help you."

When this had been achieved, the kettle was switched on and coffee and milk produced. Paula propped herself against the sink and said, "Zavvy, are you sure it's safe for you here? If anybody should come out from the house—"

"I'll do what I did this morning," he said.

"Where would you go?"

"Oh, one of the gang. Bridget I guess. She gets a bit iffy sometimes but I can trust her."

"What about her grandfather?" asked Paula, deliberately keeping her voice calm and not showing any of her own suspicions. "Do you think you can trust him too?"

"Sure. Why not? He's harmless enough."

Harmless, repeated Paula to herself. The old man's a villain, maybe even a murderer.

Aloud she said, "All the same, I don't think you ought to go there, Zavvy. It's too near this house, and too near to the clinic. You need somewhere further away, without any hassle, where you don't have to answer any questions and can really get some rest. You look awful, if you'll excuse my saying so."

"I know. They stuffed me full of dope. Supposed to be to get me off the other stuff but I think it's much worse. Anyway, I was determined to keep awake and I made myself vomit. I could do with a kip, though." He put a tea bag into a mug, poured boiling water onto it, and added three large spoonfuls of sugar. "That's better," he said after drinking. "I'm sure I can get myself off it," he added. "I know what to do and I've got the counselor at the Youth Club, but Dr. Broadbent says—"

Dr. Rose Broadbent. Paula's mind began to follow a new path.

"Why do you have to take her advice if you've got your own counselor?" she asked.

"Because she looks after them in the house here. And my Mum too. When she was alive," he added in tones of desolation before taking another drink of the hot, sweet tea.

For a few minutes there was a silence, a not unfriendly silence. Then Paula said, "Zavvy, I've got an idea. It's completely illegal and we'll both get into trouble if we're discovered, but I'm willing to risk it if you are. Do you like cats?"

"Cats?" echoed the boy in a bewildered manner. "What sort of cats? You mean the four-legged felines?"

"Yes. Two of them. Do you like them, or have you got an allergy or anything?"

"Yeah. I like them. We used to have two when Mum and I had the flat before she worked at the clinic. Siamese. Seal point."

"These aren't Siamese but they're very nice. They're at my home in Hampstead. What I'm suggesting is that we go back there tonight and you can hide for a little while until something else can be sorted out. Does that appeal?"

Paula was making herself a fresh mug of coffee as she asked the question, almost casually. When she received no immediate reply she looked up and saw that the boy was shaking his head violently and brushing a hand across his eyes.

She looked away while he shook off the threatened fit of weeping and then she said, "If you agree, then we'll go at once. I've got my car in the road but I think we'd better not go round the side of the house. It's too risky. I'll stop on the way home, though, to phone James and tell him where I am. Don't want him worrying and wondering about me. How did you get here, by the way? You didn't come through the garden, did you?"

Zavvy, now recovered, said no, he'd come through the grounds of the next-door house. He occasionally came out to the summer house that way if he didn't want to see anybody.

"When did you come?" asked Paula.

"Just now. Or rather just before I met you."

"And you didn't see anybody? And nobody saw you?"

"Not that I know of."

Then Nicholas must have gone before Zavvy arrived, thought Paula with relief.

"What about the clinic? Is it far?"

"Ten minutes' walk. I ran most of the way. Didn't meet anybody I knew."

"And you came here because you thought you could rest a while in the summer house."

It was a statement rather than a question, and Zavvy did not deny it.

"I think we'd better go out the same way," added Paula, "and we'd better go now."

She glanced at her watch. It was nearly midnight. She had been out in the garden for well over an hour, and it was odd that James had not come out from the house to look for her. What was going on there, she wondered, but she did not allow her mind to dwell on it for long. The decision to take Xavier home to Hampstead had been made on impulse, but she was not regretting it in the least, only hoping that all would go well with their getaway.

"I'm a bit scared of the dark," she said as they came to the gap in the privet hedge, "so if you don't mind, Zavvy, I'll hang on to you until we get out into the road."

10

"But where *are* you?" said James over the phone. "I've been worried sick. And when I found the car gone—"

"I'll call you when I get home," said Paula. "Can't stop now—the money's running out."

"Don't ring this number," almost shouted James. "I'll phone you. In an hour's time. One o'clock."

"Okay," said Paula and hurried out of the callbox.

When she got back to the car she found Xavier just straightening up from where he had been crouching down beside the passenger seat.

"I'm scared as a kitten," he said. "Everybody who comes by I think is looking for me. D'you think they've put me on the telly?"

"A patient discharged himself from a private clinic," said Paula thoughtfully as she switched on the engine. "No, I don't think you'd rate prime news time. Not yet."

"Not even if I was suspected of murdering my mother?"

"Did you kill your mother, Zavvy?"

"Of course I didn't. I loved the silly bitch. She's all I've got."

"I believe you. And I'd like to tell you I'm very sorry. Truly."

"Thanks. I believe *you*."

For a little while they traveled in silence. Then Paula said, "So the police didn't believe your confession?"

"It seems not. Bloody silly thing to do. Don't know why I did it."

Again there was a short silence. This time Xavier broke it.

"You don't think—you don't think somebody could have been—sort of, you know—sort of *willing* me to confess?"

"Some sort of thought control, voodoo, or whatever? Is that what you mean?"

"Yes," said the boy defiantly. "And if you think I'm mad to say so, okay then, so I am mad. Like my father."

"D'you want to talk about him?"

"Christ, no! I've had enough of that with the shrinks. But he really was. A nutter, I mean."

"Personally," said Paula choosing her words carefully. "I think it quite possible that you've been used as a scapegoat. Somebody wanted to get rid of your mother and you made a convenient suspect."

"That's what I think too."

"Do you? I'd be interested to hear."

Xavier did not respond and they drove over London Bridge and through the deserted city streets without speaking. Paula began to be afraid that he was regretting having confided in her, but when they were approaching Trafalgar Square he began to speak again.

"I've found out who started Ma on her geriatric group. It wasn't Bridget's granddad. It was Dr. Broadbent."

Paula made encouraging noises. I'll have to be very careful, she was saying to herself, not to let on what I know about Nicholas Wild. At the moment Zavvy doesn't suspect him. Maybe we can pool our knowledge later on.

Dr. Broadbent, she learned, had got Xavier's mother the job at the clinic.

"Dad was going to her clinic when he killed himself," added Zavvy. "The charity clinic, not the posh one."

Apparently Verena had not been happy at the posh clinic. It wasn't the patients, poor buggers, it was the staff.

"This guy was always getting at her, said she was stupid and clumsy, which she is—I mean, she was, poor cow."

It didn't take long for Paula to realize that "this guy" was Kevin Casey.

"But he didn't like it when she left and got a housekeeping job," added Zavvy. "Neither did Dr. Broadbent. Neither did I. They treated us both like muck."

From a somewhat confused narrative Paula learned that Verena had been in two other jobs, staying only a few weeks in each, before she came to the Macgregors.

"She saw the advertisement, I suppose," said Paula.

Xavier thought that Dr. Broadbent had pointed it out to her, but he couldn't really remember much about that time. He'd had problems of his own. Paula didn't ask what they were, but said she was glad his mother found something that suited her. Xavier responded by saying that he thought the generation-gap business was silly, but Bridget was keen on it and so was her grandfather.

"And it was Dr. Broadbent who suggested it," said Paula. "What do you think of Dr. Broadbent, Zavvy?"

The boy's reply was rather confused. "She was okay when I—when I really needed help. I guess she's a good doctor."

"But you don't like her posh clinic?"

"It's different. It's sort of—you know—sort of—it's like—"

"They give you overlarge doses of drugs?" suggested Paula.

"Yeah. I guess that's it. And they watch you. All the time."

"How do you mean? Surely you have a room to yourself?"

"There's an eye in the door. There's always someone watching you. It sends you crazy."

Zavvy's voice was trembling. Paula decided that it would be wise to change the subject.

"It's not much further," she said. "We're coming up to Hampstead Heath now. Do you ever come to this part of London?"

There was no reply. Paula, temporarily stopped at a traffic light, glanced at Xavier and saw that his eyes were closed and he looked completely exhausted. Once she got home he woke up sufficiently to stumble out of the car and into the house, and there was a slight return of animation when the cats arrived and tried to climb up his legs. But when she took him to one of the spare rooms and was suggesting that he might like to borrow some of James's things, he suddenly gave a huge yawn and a moment later was lying across the bed, dead to the world.

Paula, wishing that she could be in the same condition but feeling much too agitated to rest, went downstairs to make more coffee and wait for James's phone call.

"Can we talk?" she asked cautiously as soon as she heard his voice.

"Okay this end. What about you?"

"No problem. Sorry I can't tell you more about it at this moment, but I've made a solemn promise. I've been helping somebody who badly needs help. It'll all come out tomorrow. But what I can tell you now is this."

Quickly she related her activities in the garden up to the moment when Kevin and Nicholas Wild departed. James listened without interrupting.

"So that's where Kevin had got to," he said when Paula had finished. "Dr. Broadbent was asking for him, but we couldn't—"

"She's in it too," interrupted Paula. "I'm sure she is."

"How do you know?"

"I don't know. I suspect," said Paula, remembering her promise to Zavvy. "Do go on. What's been happening? How's Aunt Isobel?"

"Fast asleep. Presumably no worse than usual."

"And Uncle Mac?"

"Absolutely furious because I'd summoned the doctor without telling him. We had quite a row about it, right there in Auntie's room. Actually Aunt Isobel was enjoying it. She loves a bit of drama."

"And Dr. Rose?"

"She was furious too, but she hid it better than poor old Mac. Made a pretense of examining Aunt Isobel, said that what she needed was some rest, and had she enough of her sleeping pills left, or did she need a fresh prescription, and so on and so forth. At that point Uncle Mac remembered his devoted husband act and said he would fetch her pills."

James paused.

"Go on, go on," said Paula.

"Aunt Isobel stopped him," continued James with a laugh. "She produced the bottle from under the pillow and took out one of her sleeping tablets and picked up her glass of water and looked around at all of us in the way she sometimes does, very alert, and said very clearly, 'Has anybody poisoned this? Am I safe in drinking it?' "

"Good for her," said Paula. "What next, James?"

"Uncle Mac nearly exploded. Dr. Broadbent looked daggers."

"And you?"

"If I hadn't been there I think they'd have whisked her

back to the clinic as a patient suffering from acute persecution mania."

"She wouldn't have dared to behave like that if you hadn't been there," said Paula.

"Probably not. Anyway, I decided it was time to take a hand. I took the glass away from her and went over to the wash basin and rinsed it out very thoroughly and poured in fresh water. Then I brought it back to her and told her to show me the sleeping tablets. She gave me the bottle and they looked all right, but I hung on to it and I said to Uncle Mac and the doctor, 'Will you please assure me that these are her normal tablets. We don't want anything happening to my aunt, do we?'—or some such words."

Paula was listening with delight. "I do wish I'd been there," she said. "They must have been absolutely steaming."

"You can say that again. They'd have had *me* in the clinic too, if they could. But I've burned my boats, Paula, my love. It's open warfare now," he added in much more serious tones, "and it's a very good thing that you are safely out of it."

"But I'm coming back tomorrow—or do you think I ought not to?"

"How do you feel about it yourself?" countered James.

"Of course I want to come. I want to keep a watch on what you are given to eat," added Paula, and she was only half-joking.

"At least Kevin will be gone tomorrow," said James.

"He won't, you know. He's got his orders to stay. I told you. And Uncle Mac will make sure that he does stay."

"Damn. You're right. What are we going to do?"

"I think we ought to get Aunt Isobel out of that house at once."

"You're dead right. As usual. A reputable nursing home. Somewhere in Hampstead. Near us."

"Absolutely."

They agreed that James should suggest it to Aunt Isobel as soon as she awoke, and Paula promised to be with him as soon as she could settle her own problem.

But what on earth am I to do with Zavvy, she asked herself when she went to bed at last. She spent a long time worrying about that and about everything else, so that the dawn was already breaking when at last sleep came to her.

She was awakened by a knock on the door. The bedside clock said nearly nine, and brilliant sunshine was filling the room. Feeling completely disoriented, she called out, "Come in."

A tall thin boy in his late teens stood there holding a tray on which was a plate of biscuits and a mug.

"I made tea," said Xavier, speaking very carefully and correctly. "I couldn't figure out how to use the coffee grinder. And I fed the cats. There was a tin of cat food already opened in the fridge. Was that okay? Oh shit," he added in his normal manner after he had put down the tray.

"What's the matter?" asked Paula.

"I forgot the sugar."

"I never take it," said Paula, and proceeded to express her thanks.

Fifteen minutes later they were sitting at the kitchen table, eating cornflakes and discussing what to do.

"I liked Bridget very much," said Paula, after Zavvy had made a few desultory suggestions, "but I do most definitely think you ought to keep right away from anybody connected with the Macgregors."

"I don't see how I can," objected Zavvy. "I was supposed to stay in the clinic. They'll have told the police I've gone."

"I'm not so sure about that." Paula thought for a moment.

"Listen, I know I promised that I wouldn't tell anyone you were with me, but I think we really do need help now. So do you mind if I tell James? He can find out what's been happening at the clinic and sort it all out with the police if need be."

Xavier was looking at her in a puzzled manner. "Yeah, you promised me, but I didn't think you really meant it. You mean you really *meant* it—that you wouldn't tell anybody?"

"Of course I meant it," snapped Paula. "If I promise to do something then I do it, if it's humanly possible."

"I don't get it," said the boy, shaking his head. "It just isn't—I don't get it. It isn't—"

Words failed him. Paula reached for the telephone.

"James? Thank heaven it's you," she said a moment later. "Where are you?"

"In the sitting room, on my own," he replied. "Aunt Isobel's still asleep and Kevin and Uncle Mac are in conference in the kitchen, I *think*, but if you've something urgent to tell me you'd better wait while I go to a callbox—damn nuisance not having a mobile phone, but I don't trust anybody in this house."

"Neither do I. Okay, I'll wait."

Five minutes later Paula was explaining, very briefly, about Xavier. "If you could sort out his position and call me back, then I'll stay here till you call. And if there's no problem, then he can stay here and look after the house and the cats. I'll introduce him to a few people in the road so they know he's meant to be here."

"Is he with you at this moment?"

"No. He's raiding that heap of old clothes you chucked out for charity. A slight change of image to suit Heathview Villas is called for. I think we can trust him, James."

"On your head be it if he becamps with our most cherished possessions."

"It wouldn't be in his own interest."

"No, that's our main security. But what about his friends?"

"That's the worst risk, that he'll start calling up people, but I think it's very unlikely. I think I can put it to him in such a way—honestly I don't think we're taking much risk. And he really loves cats."

"So did some of the worst villains the world has ever seen," said James gloomily. "I'll have to go now. Don't like being away from the house for long."

A few minutes later Xavier appeared in the front hall. Paula surveyed him with satisfaction.

"You look positively distinguished," she said. "Leisure wear for the rising young executive. I thought James's things might fit you."

"I feel bloody silly," said the boy.

"Have you ever done any acting?" demanded Paula.

"Well, yes. Sort of."

"Where?" she asked.

Reluctantly he admitted to having played quite a big role in a most ambitious Youth Club production of a Harold Pinter play.

"Right," said Paula briefly. "Then this is your role for Heathview Villas. You're one of James's students and you're staying here because—because—"

"He's giving me some extra tutoring in return for some work in the garden and some decorating in the house, and—"

"I've no need to suggest anything," interrupted Paula. "It's all yours, Zavvy, so long as you know your story."

By the time James telephoned again Zavvy had thoroughly rehearsed his act, had been introduced to the neighbors, and had made a list of the jobs that he proposed to do in the house and garden. When Paula remarked that they didn't really expect him to do much, he looked quite offended. She was hastily assuring him that they would be very grateful when the phone rang.

"Okay for him to stay," said James abruptly, and added, "Is he there? I'd like to speak to him."

Paula handed over the phone. Curiosity was urging her to go and listen on the extension in the hall, but tact forbade. Xavier was turning out to have some very good qualities, and she felt more and more friendly towards him, but there was no doubt that he could be very touchy. This phone call was obviously to be regarded as a man-to-man thing and she would just have to wait to learn what it was about.

At last it was finished and he said quietly, "James says tell Paula he can't wait to see her." Then suddenly he burst out laughing, did a vault over the back of the sofa, collapsed onto it again and continued to laugh uncontrollably.

Paula glared at him for a moment and then without speaking turned round and proceeded to walk towards the door. This tactic worked.

"I'm sorry," called out Zavvy. "Please don't go away."

Paula turned round. "Have you anything to tell me?" she asked coldly.

"Yes," he replied meekly. "It's very bizarre. They've had the police at the clinic, but nothing to do with me." He began to laugh again. Paula waited in silence until he had controlled himself.

"But it is drugs," he said, switching into his sober and responsible role. "They think it's a distribution center. They even suspect Dr. Rose's boyfriend. He's the guy who runs the place. Everybody's being questioned. Nobody cares whether I'm there or not or what becomes of me," he added with a lapse into resentment and self-pity.

"That's fine," said Paula briskly. "No problem. You're all

ours. Are you sure you'll be all right here on your own?" she added with sudden misgiving.

"Yeah. I'll be fine."

He was barely listening to her. He was looking at the bookshelves, at the desk on which James's personal computer stood. He wanted her to be gone.

At the door Paula couldn't resist asking, "Zavvy, if there really is some sort of drug ring operating from the clinic, do you think Dr. Broadbent is part of it?"

"Who knows?" he replied, his mind still obviously on his own plans for the day. "Who knows?"

11

Paula parked her red mini outside the empty house next to the Macgregors. She picked up the case in which she had packed a few things for herself and James, plus the morning's mail, and stood hesitantly under one of the chestnut trees at the side of the road. In broad daylight the empty house looked sad rather than sinister. The front garden was a tangle of unpruned rose bushes, the gravel path was full of weeds, the wooden gate had a broken hinge and one end of it was dragging on the ground.

The Secret Garden, said Paula to herself, recollecting a much-loved book from childhood. But that had had a happy ending. Were there to be any happy endings to this affair in which she and James were now involved? For Xavier, perhaps. She seemed to have established a good relationship with him, and no doubt James would do the same. Had the boy got staying power as well as talent? Was there any chance at all of his becoming a professional actor?

What he needed, decided Paula, was the right woman in his life. Not his poor silly mother. Bridget perhaps. The girl had possibilities, but it was difficult now to think of her except in connection with that wicked old grandfather of hers, who seemed to be very familiar with this empty house whose garden Paula was now staring at.

An artist. Possibly a forger. Even a thief.

Paula moved nearer to the sagging gate, her imagination building pictures of secret studios hidden within the crumbling old mansion. She was actually standing looking over the gate when the front door opened and down the stone steps came two men. One of them was youngish, dark-suited, slick-looking. Estate agent, was Paula's instant verdict. The other was old and shabby, the very man she had been thinking about.

There was no hiding behind a rhododendron bush this time, no pretending that she had not been standing there staring at the house.

"Well, well," said Nicholas Wild, coming forward to greet her. "If it isn't the lady professor. Could it be that we have a rival purchaser here, Mr. Parkinson?"

The slick man moved nearer to Paula. "Are you interested in buying a property? If so—" he produced a card—"my firm is—"

Paula interrupted, hastily disclaiming any such intention. "It reminded me of a book I used to love as a child," she added. "I'm afraid I was just standing here dreaming."

"*The Secret Garden*," said the estate agent, surprising Paula. "I used to love it too."

They smiled at each other, a strange little moment of genuine human contact between two complete strangers who would surely never meet again.

"Sentimental twaddle," said Nicholas Wild brusquely. "Well, Mr. Parkinson, I don't think I need to keep you any longer. You'll be hearing from my solicitors."

"Thank you, sir," said the estate agent, holding open the gate. "We look forward to receiving your offer."

Taking no further notice of Paula, the two men walked

towards a black Ford Sierra that was parked a few yards down the road. Belatedly Paula told herself that she ought to have noted who the estate agents were, for there was no board on the premises, and then she realized that she was in fact holding the card. "Broadbent and Freeman," it read, with an address not far from Barley Avenue.

Broadbent. Like Dr. Rose. There need not be any connection. It might well be the name of a partner long since dead, but it was not a particularly common name, and Paula found it impossible not to start speculating.

If James could pretend he was interested in buying, Paula said to herself, then perhaps we could explore. As she was thinking this, suddenly James was by her side, having been looking out of the window next door, very impatient to talk to her.

"Sorry," she said, "but it's so extraordinary—"

"And I've got something extraordinary to tell you. Come on. Let's get into my car. What's that? Oh yes. Today's mail. Let's pretend we're looking at it. I don't trust *anybody*—less than ever now. Do hurry *up*, Paula."

He grabbed at the little suitcase, pulled out some of the envelopes that she had laid on top, and let the case and its contents slide to the floor of the car. His impatience was infectious. Paula spread out a long list of items now available at an antiquarian bookseller's and they both appeared to be poring over it, deeply interested.

"It's a book," murmured James. "One of Grandpa's."

Paula, momentarily confused, actually found herself noticing one or two of the items on the list.

"In manuscript, never published," James continued in the same conspiratorial whisper. "Grandpa gave it to Aunt Isobel and told her to keep it."

"When?" muttered Paula, now completely alert.

"All of sixty years ago—before he became famous. Early work. He said he didn't want it published. But now—"

"It's worth a fortune," interrupted Paula, with difficulty suppressing her excitement. "An entirely unknown work by G.E. Goff! James—darling James—" and her fingers dug into his arm. "It's like finding a completely new Thomas Hardy. Or Virginia Woolf. The libraries! The museums! And whoever publishes it!"

Her voice had risen, despite herself. James, stretching out his left leg, gave her ankle a sharp kick.

"Sorry," he muttered as she protested, "but we *must* be careful." He turned over a page of the catalogue they were pretending to study. "Kevin's around. I've just seen him in the mirror. He's on the front doorstep, pretending to be polishing the brass knocker."

"Does he know you know?"

"Not yet, though he probably suspects. He's trying to stop me from taking Auntie away to our place or to a nursing home. So is Uncle Mac. I've fixed with the Hampstead one provisionally, but she won't come unless she can bring *it* with her."

"Bring the—?" broke in Paula.

"Yes. Don't say anything."

"But where is it?"

"She won't tell me. Come on." James folded up the bookseller's list, collected the scattered papers and put them into the suitcase. He got out of the car. "Thanks for bringing this," he said clearly as they moved towards the Macgregors' front gate, "I'll try to get an answer drafted today if there's time."

Kevin, still rubbing at the brass knocker, moved aside to let them enter the house. He made no attempt to greet Paula, but she could feel his animosity. He's worried, she said to herself. His boss isn't pleased with him. He's no nearer finding that manuscript than we are. If Aunt Isobel would only trust me—

"How is your aunt?" she asked James, loud enough for Kevin to hear.

"Not too bad," he replied. "I believe she's asleep at the moment, but maybe later on—"

"I'd like to see her when she feels up to it," said Paula.

They were going upstairs now, making conversation for Kevin's benefit. Though we really don't need to trouble, thought Paula, because it's open war now, as James says himself.

"And where is Uncle Mac?" she asked as they reached the door of their room.

James made no reply until they had entered and closed the door behind them. Then he collapsed onto the bed, pulled Paula down beside him, and clung to her. He began to laugh and seemed unable to stop.

"My b-bloody grandfather!" he said at last. "I wish he'd been a coal miner or a dustman. Famous novelist my arse! He was nothing but trouble to everybody all his life, and years after his death he's still causing trouble. One murder and one criminal conspiracy and God knows what's still to come. I don't *care* that he was a genius. He hated me and I hated him and—oh, Paula, Paula, darling Paula, I'm terribly sorry but it's stirred it all up again, what he did to my parents and—and—"

Paula, her mind floating with memories, did her best to soothe him.

"Sorry," he said at last, standing up and moving restlessly about the room. "Of course it's wonderful that there'll be a totally unknown work by G.E. Goff. Literature comes first and all the rest of it."

"It doesn't come first," said Paula firmly. "Aunt Isobel comes first. How are we going to get her away?"

"She has agreed in principle," replied James, "but not without the manuscript, and she won't tell me where it is."

"Why?" demanded Paula.

"I suppose she doesn't trust me."

"Trust you—in what way?"

"Not to make it public. But dammit," continued James angrily as he began to prowl around again, "it's mine by rights. I ought to have been his heir."

"Of course you ought," said Paula, "but there's not much point in going over that now. After all, we're still not entirely sure that the manuscript exists. I mean, isn't it possible that Aunt Isobel is making it all up, that she really is—"

James interrupted with the words that, to spare his feelings, she had hesitated to say.

"That she's just plain crazy. Senile dementia, paranoia—anything you like to call it."

Paula nodded without speaking.

"In which case," he went on, "Uncle Mac and Dr. Rose and Kevin and the rest of them were perfectly justified in putting her into the clinic, and everybody is acting purely in the best interests of my crazy old aunt. There's no conspiracy, there's no hidden treasure."

James shook his head sadly. "It's no go, love. It won't wash. I'd like to believe it but it isn't true. I don't say she isn't a bit mad—of course she is. All the Goffs are mad except me. But there is most certainly a conspiracy. Even if this damned manuscript doesn't exist, there are people who firmly believe that it does and are determined to get hold of it. Have you forgotten your nice old artist friend and his midnight chat with Kevin?"

Paula answered with a question. "Tell me truly, James, do you yourself believe that this manuscript exists?"

"Yes, I do," he replied without hesitation. "It's just the

sort of thing my grandfather would do. He wasn't satisfied with it but he didn't want to revise it and he could never bear to throw anything away. Neither can Aunt Isobel. He gave it to her to keep and he knew he could get it back whenever he wanted it. But he never did want it during his years of fame, and Auntie never reminded him. In fact he quarreled with her too. They weren't on speaking terms for years. That's why she wouldn't cooperate with you when you were writing your book."

"I never found the slightest hint of this manuscript," said Paula, "but I'll have to take your word for it that it exists. After all, there've been other unexpected literary discoveries. The Byron letters, for instance."

She stood up. "Okay, we've got two big objectives. Protect your aunt comes first, finding the manuscript comes second. Where do we go from here?"

"Rose Broadbent, I think," said James. "She came in this morning and I actually managed to get her on her own for a few minutes. That clinic of hers is owned and run by her boyfriend, who is a very eminent psychiatrist, and it looks as if he's been running a lucrative little drug racket as well. I don't think Kevin or Verena can be involved in it. Apparently it's very recent, quite a time after those two left the clinic, but Dr. Rose is certainly involved, whether or not she is actually guilty of anything herself. So, my dearest Paula, she is in a somewhat difficult position, and is very open to a little judicious bullying or even blackmail."

"Excellent," said Paula. "Is she coming back here today?"

"She said she'd look in this afternoon. I suspect it's as much to find out what I'm up to as to visit the sickroom. There's the bell now." James hurried to the door.

"What do you want me to do?" Paula called after him.

"Work on Aunt Isobel. Good luck."

He pulled open the door. At the same moment Kevin

came running downstairs from the top floor and Uncle Mac appeared in the doorway of Aunt Isobel's bedroom. Paula, keeping out of sight, heard him say to James, "Aren't you gone yet?" and then call out to Kevin to go and answer the front doorbell.

James said loudly that he had no intention of leaving the house and that he wanted to speak to the doctor. Uncle Mac retorted in similar tones that it was none of James's business. Kevin joined in, and Paula, still hidden, could hear the three of them shouting at each other as they went downstairs.

Aunt Isobel's room was across the landing. Paula ran to the door, pulled it open without knocking, shut it behind her, found the key in the lock, and turned it.

They can bang on that door all night, she said to herself, but I'm not going to open it until I've got out of Aunt Isobel where that manuscript is. As James says, this is open war, and this is my part of the battlefield.

She checked the key again and turned round to look into the room. For a moment she thought her action had been in vain. The bed was made up and there was no sign of the old lady. And then, just as on an earlier occasion, she saw Aunt Isobel's face peering round the side of the big green chair that stood in front of the bay window.

Paula ran towards her, knelt down beside the chair, took hold of the old woman's hands, and said gently, "Aunt Isobel—James and I want you to come to Hampstead for a little while so that we can take care of you. Either in our house with a nurse, or in a nearby nursing home. Please come. We want you to. Very much indeed."

Paula was looking closely into the old face as she spoke. It looked more shrunken than ever and there was fear in the faded eyes. But for a moment, as she was speaking, she was convinced that she saw a favorable reaction, a little light of longing and hope.

She wants to come. I know she does, said Paula to herself. I'm just not going to believe her if she refuses.

"Will you come?" she said quietly but firmly. "James will arrange it all. There won't be any trouble here. And you can bring with you anything you want to."

The hands that she was holding began to tremble; the obstinate look returned to the old woman's face.

"I can't come without—" she began breathlessly.

"James has told me," interrupted Paula. "You must bring the manuscript with you. Tell me where it is and we will see that it is kept safely."

Aunt Isobel's reply was so soft that Paula had to bend even closer to hear.

"I don't know where it is."

For a moment Paula's skepticism returned in full force. It doesn't exist, she said to herself. Then immediately she thought, I'm going to believe that it does. James believes it.

"Where and when did you last see it?" she asked.

The answer came with surprising firmness. "About ten days ago. When I took it from—from where I used to keep it."

"Why did you take it?"

"Because I thought they were looking for it."

"Who was looking for it."

"Mac, of course." Her tone was sharp and irritable, as if Paula had asked a foolish question. "He won't kill me until he's got hold of it."

Again Paula's doubts rose to the surface. Was the old woman really sane? Was the whole thing the invention of a disturbed mind?

No, no, no, she scolded herself. She's frightened and

muddled and sometimes quite unbalanced, but the gist of it is true, we know it's true.

"So what did you do with it?" she asked, "after you took it from wherever . . . ?"

The answer came quickly and clearly.

"I gave it to Xavier. Verena's boy."

"To Zavvy!" Paula was so surprised that her voice rose in spite of herself. Quickly she regained control. "Why did you give it to him?" she asked quietly.

"Because there was nobody else I could trust," she replied.

Paula was so astonished that she could not immediately think what to say or do. She was spared the decision by the sound of somebody banging on the door. She got up and walked towards it. "Who's that?" she called out.

James's voice answered. "Sorry to interrupt, but it isn't the doctor. It's Inspector Martin, and he'd like to ask you a few questions about when you found Verena in the summer house."

12

Paula unlocked the door. There was no alternative. To her great relief she saw that James was alone.

"Auntie gave it to Zavvy," she whispered, "for safekeeping because she felt she could trust him. You stay here, tell her that Zavvy is at our home, and I'm sure she'll come. Good luck."

James seemed to recover from astonishment more quickly than Paula had done, but there was something else on his mind.

"If the Inspector asks about Zavvy," he murmured.

"I shall tell him where he is," she replied firmly.

"And the—the precious object? I've said nothing."

"Then neither shall I. After all, we don't really know."

"Good luck then."

Three men turned to look at Paula as she came into the big sitting room. In the eyes of Uncle Mac and Kevin there was unconcealed hostility, but the police inspector, middle-aged and weary-looking, regarded her with indifference.

"I won't keep you long, Professor Glenning," he said.

"I'm sorry I wasn't available when you came before," said Paula.

They both turned to the other two, expecting them to leave the room. Neither moved.

"Is there somewhere we can talk in private?" said Inspector Martin to Uncle Mac.

"You'd better stay here," said the old man curtly. "Come on, Kevin. I need to talk to you."

After they had gone Paula turned to look at the police inspector again and decided that, uninterested though he might appear, he was in fact well aware of the atmosphere of tension in the house. I wish I could ask him what they know or suspect, she thought as she sat down.

"You and Dr. Goff found Mrs. Keeling unconscious at—roughly what time?" he asked.

With some difficulty Paula recalled the events of that first night at the Macgregors' house.

Zavvy had tried to shock Aunt Isobel. She had snubbed him very neatly, and he had taken it well, which would seem to confirm that there was no real enmity, but in fact some sort of understanding between them.

Paula did not say this aloud to the inspector. "Mrs. Macgregor became ill," she said, "and her husband said he would help her to bed. He asked Verena—Mrs. Keeling—to bring her some warm milk later. Mrs. Keeling left the room and did not return at all. Mrs. Macgregor was afraid she had said something to upset her, and asked if Dr. Goff and I would go after her and reassure her. We didn't know where she had gone, and at first we went into the kitchen, then into all the other rooms and also up to the housekeeper's rooms on the top floor."

"How long did you spend looking for her?" asked Inspector Martin.

"Quite a long time," replied Paula. "We weren't very keen on the errand, and we rather wanted a chance to talk. We were much more anxious about Dr. Goff's aunt than about Mrs. Keeling. It must have been at least twenty minutes."

"And you actually found her in the summer house," prompted the inspector. "How long after she left the room was that?"

Paula thought for a moment before replying. These were the vital minutes, she said to herself. During that time—shall we say twenty minutes?—somebody came into the summer house and hit Verena on the head. Or she downed some more drinks and fell and hit herself.

"I'm sorry I can't be more exact," she said aloud, "but I think it must have been twenty or twenty-five minutes between the time Mrs. Keeling left the room and the time that Dr. Goff and I found her unconscious."

"And before she left the room—when you were here together and Mrs. Macgregor became ill—what was your impression of Mrs. Keeling's state of mind and of her behavior?"

"I'd only just met her for the first time," Paula reminded him.

"Yes, I realize that. But you must have formed some impression."

"I thought she was—not very sensible," replied Paula. "Not self-controlled. I didn't think she was a very suitable companion for an old lady."

"Not controlled. In what way?"

"Well, frankly it occurred to me that she could be a heavy drinker."

"Thank you."

He made a note. Paula felt sure that he had heard this before. Have they firm evidence, she asked herself, that Verena's fatal injury was, or was not, caused by accident?

"Was that the cause of her death?" she asked impulsively. "Did she trip and fall and hurt her head?"

"It's not impossible," said Inspector Martin wearily. "Just one more question. I believe that her son—" he paused to consult his notes and stumbled over the name—"Xavier was present when Mrs. Macgregor became ill. Did he depart before or after his mother?"

"Before," replied Paula instantly. "And he left the house. We heard the front door bang loudly."

"Do you know where he went?"

"I've no idea."

"You know he made a confession?"

"I was told so. And that he was later released. I've never quite understood why. May I ask you why, Inspector Martin?"

"Certainly you may. There is no secret about it. He went straight to the home of his friend Miss Bridget Wild," was the reply. "I believe you know her, Professor Glenning."

"Yes indeed. She and her grandfather were kind enough to invite me to breakfast yesterday morning."

"According to Miss Wild, Mr. Keeling remained with them for about fifteen minutes, very restless and distressed, and then said he'd better go back and see if his mother was all right. He'd said something to upset her and was feeling bad about it. He was also concerned about the old lady who had been taken ill. When he returned here he intended to come round to the back of the house, thinking his mother could let him in at the back door, but he saw the lights on in the summer house at the end of the garden and he went straight there instead."

"And he found me there, with his mother unconscious," said Paula. "Dr. Goff had gone to tell Mr. Macgregor and call a doctor, and later they both came back with the doctor."

"Yes. What was your own impression when you found Mrs. Keeling?"

Paula answered as honestly as she could. So that's

Zavvy's alibi, she was saying to herself. Bridget and her grandfather. Both of them? All the time? All of those vital twenty minutes? But Bridget thought he could have hit his mother *before* he went to her. And so he could. He could be lying and lying. He's a good actor.

Inspector Martin thanked her for her help and stood up to leave. Then he spoke again, and for the first time since she had seen him Paula thought she could detect a flicker of a smile.

"I hope you will find young Mr. Keeling satisfactory as an odd job man about the house," he said.

The smile became broader at the sight of Paula's surprise.

"How do we know? Because he phoned us himself. We released him on condition that he keeps us informed of his movements, which he has done."

"I suppose I ought to have told you myself that he had left the clinic," said Paula. "My excuse must be that the whole business was totally unexpected and I'm still not at all sure that I've done the right thing."

"Time alone will tell," said the inspector sententiously as he moved to the door.

Paula followed him into the hall and stood there for a moment or two after he had left the house. She could hear no sound of movement nor of voices. Presumably James was still with Aunt Isobel. But where were Kevin and Uncle Mac?

She took a step in the direction of the kitchen and then changed her mind. What she wanted above all at this moment was to speak to Zavvy. Her mind was flooding with questions. Why, if he was so willing to let the police know his movements, had he been so frightened last night after running away from the clinic? She had assumed that it was the police he was afraid of, but obviously it was something or somebody else. Had the whole business of making a confession been intended to get himself arrested and thus ensure his own protection?

But from whom? Surely not from Nicholas Wild. He had gone from the Macgregors' house to Bridget's on the night his mother died. And to go to Bridget's meant to go to Nicholas. Here was something that Paula needed to know from Zavvy. When he took refuge with Bridget, was Nicholas there? All the time? In that case Nicholas, too, had an alibi for those vital twenty minutes.

"I've simply got to speak to Zavvy," Paula muttered to herself. "Dare I risk a phone call?"

She decided against it. James had gone out to the public callbox when he wanted to talk to her.

Paula opened the front door and then hesitated again. She didn't want James to worry about her, but she also did not want to go upstairs and get caught up in whatever was going on; not just at this moment. And she had no key to the house, so if she shut the front door she could not get in again. On the other hand, one could usually get in at the back. The kitchen door seemed to be left unlocked when there were people about.

She ran down the steps and along to the callbox and waited impatiently for her call to be answered. At last a strange, high-pitched male voice said, "What number are you calling?"

Anxiously, irritably, Paula spoke her own phone number.

"Sorry," said Zavvy in his own voice, "but I thought I'd better be careful. Everything's okay here, though, and I called the police to let them know where I was."

"Yes, I know. So why all the hiding away last night if you didn't care if the police found you?"

"If you don't mind, Paula, I'd rather not talk about it over the phone."

"Fair enough, but can you answer me this?"

Quickly Paula put her other question, which Zavvy answered readily enough.

"Grandpa came in while I was talking to Bridget. Can't remember exactly when. B. wasn't pleased with me. Told me off for being nasty to Mama. We were sort of quarreling."

And the next morning, thought Paula, they were still quarreling because Bridget thought Zavvy had actually hit his mother.

"Did you speak to her grandfather yourself?" she asked.

"No. He wasn't in the mood. He came upstairs and looked at me and grunted and then went into his own room and slammed the door."

"And then?"

"We resumed our quarrel, less enthusiastically. I'd been hoping to stay the night. Didn't feel like going back to the squat where I've got some of my worldly possessions, but B. wasn't encouraging, so in the end I decided I'd better come back and be nice to my Mum, and then maybe Bridget, but—"

He stopped speaking suddenly.

And you found your mother unconscious and dying, Paula finished for him in her mind, and Bridget, really worried, came after you and accused you.

"Thanks, Zavvy," she said aloud. "Just wanted to get it straight."

"Have you seen Bridget today?"

"Not yet, but I'm going to try to see her as soon as I can. I don't think we'll be back tonight, though it's just possible. Are you sure you're all right on your own?"

"Fine, but I do wish you would try to see Bridget. She's got some things of mine that I didn't want to leave in the squat. Everything gets nicked there."

"Some things of yours?" echoed Paula, controlling her

rising excitement. Things. That must surely include the manuscript—if it existed and if it was true that Aunt Isobel had given it to Zavvy for safekeeping. The precious manuscript. In the house of the very man who was trying to get hold of it!

"It's an old canvas zip bag," Zavvy was saying. "Dark blue, very dirty. B. put it in her cupboard."

"I'll go round at once," said Paula, "and bring it to you this evening. I can tell you're worried about it."

It was on the tip of her tongue to ask if it contained something that Aunt Isobel had given him, but she restrained herself. It was not wise to talk about it on the phone. Zavvy sounded anxious about it, but not in the state of near hysteria that was threatening her. It was more than likely that he knew he had something that was of value to Aunt Isobel, but very unlikely that he knew of its great potential value to whoever could get hold of it. Otherwise he would surely have mentioned it to her before.

Paula replaced the phone with this conviction in her mind, but almost instantly her thoughts turned right over again. She asked herself, But suppose Zavvy did know? Suppose that was the reason he had been so afraid, because he knew that somebody was trying to get hold of it.

He's no fool, thought Paula; in fact he's very bright. Suppose Zavvy did know and was playing his own game, playing it very cool as he knew well how to do: making it sound as if he was worried but not excessively so; not knowing that Paula knew what was in that bag, but manipulating her into retrieving it for him. And if she did retrieve it and take it up to him in Hampstead, what were the odds that he would remain in their house after she had departed again?

13

"I've got to stop wondering if Zavvy knows about the manuscript," said Paula to herself as she came out of the call-box.

Whatever the truth might be, she must get hold of that canvas bag as soon as she possibly could and have a look at its contents. And then she and James could decide together what to do next.

She got into her car and drove to the end of Barley Avenue. The greengrocer's shop—did one turn right or left? With an effort she recalled the way that Bridget had driven her. Please let Bridget be there and on her own, she prayed. Would she have to go through the shop to get into the house, or was there another entrance? And could she escape Nicholas? She had last seen him negotiating with the estate agent, not so very long ago. Perhaps he might not have gone straight home; or perhaps it was early closing day for the shops in that area.

Perhaps anything, except that she would have to encounter Nicholas Wild on her own, because all the excuses and explanations that she could think of sounded hopelessly feeble, and she knew that he was already suspicious of her.

Paula found the shop without difficulty and also found a

parking place nearby. The shutters were down and there was no sign of life, although the other little shops in the street were all open and doing business.

Alongside the greengrocer's shop there was a door that looked as if it was part of the same premises. It was painted dark green and looked both depressing and uninviting. Paula took a step towards it and then changed her mind. On the other side of the greengrocer's she had noticed a small news agent's. Why not go in and buy an evening paper and some cigarettes? News agents' shops were chatty places. With luck she might learn something about the people next door.

At first it looked as if she was not going to have any luck. The proprietor, a thin, mournful-looking Welshman, was occupied with a customer who was protesting about the non-delivery of his Sunday papers. Two younger men, who looked as if they had been working on a building site, were standing impatiently behind. After about half a minute they both picked up evening papers and left some money on the counter. The proprietor and his angry customer continued their argument.

Paula stood staring at a shelf full of small items of stationery as if it had a great attraction for her, and was rewarded for her patience by the sound of a woman's voice inquiring if she needed any help. It was a bright, lively voice and its owner looked just the sort of person Paula had hoped to encounter—a short, plump, middle-aged woman with a friendly smile and very alert dark eyes.

"I'm looking for envelopes." Paula hastily invented a need. "But I can't see any the right size."

"We don't get much demand for the bigger ones," said the woman, hunting through some boxes that stood on the floor, "but there might be some downstairs."

Paula, conscience striking her, hastily stopped the obliging woman from searching for unwanted items, and asked instead for cigarettes.

"Oh, and a birthday card," she added. "I've just remembered."

She actually did want to buy a birthday card and the choosing of it took a little time and naturally led to some conversation. By the time the purchase had been made the news agent had got rid of his awkward customer and was serving others who had come into the shop, while Paula and his wife were chatting about the weather, the locality, and the prosperity or otherwise of the shops in the area.

"I noticed a greengrocer," said Paula, "but they're shut."

"They're shut half the time," said the news agent's wife in disapproving tones. "If you ask me, it's simply a coverup for something else."

"That sounds very intriguing," said Paula. "What do you think it could be?"

"It's the cars," said the news agent's wife. "Not the sort you'd expect to see at a little place like that. Brand new Mercs, a nineteen-thirties Rolls in super condition—that was a beauty!—and driven by a woman too. She came in here for some cigarettes."

"How lovely," said Paula. "I've only got a mini."

She had hoped for further revelations, but her words were drowned by a sudden burst of sound from the radio of a van that had stopped just outside the shop. The woman was obliged to attend to a rush of customers. In any case, thought Paula, there was probably not much more to be learned here.

Nicholas Wild was certainly not a hardworking shopkeeper who depended on his business for a living. That she already knew. People driving expensive cars came and stopped at his shop. That she had not known, but was not surprised to hear.

As she came away from the news agent's she noticed a car being maneuvered into an empty space near the greengrocer's. It was an old Rover, a reliable family car with nothing special about it. The driver, a middle-aged man, looked as if there was nothing special about him either.

Paula, having decided that there was no alternative to direct action, arrived at the dark green door at the same time as he did. They glanced at each other in a mildly curious but not unfriendly manner, and then she said, "I can't see any bell."

"Neither can I. But there's a letterbox."

With some difficulty he succeeded in pushing at the flap so that it made a rattling sound.

"Do you know Mr. Wild?" asked Paula as they waited.

"Not at all. He's on my list for a home visit. I'm a doctor. A locum, as a matter of fact."

"I'm trying to see his granddaughter," said Paula. "I don't think anybody heard us. Let's try again."

They tried, and half a minute later the door was opened by a distraught and apologetic Bridget, who clutched at the doctor and apparently did not even notice Paula standing on the doorstep behind him.

"I can't keep him quiet," cried Bridget, dragging the doctor into the house. "He keeps trying to get up and swears he'll kill that driver."

Still talking excitedly, she hurried him along the ill-lit passage. Neither of them stayed to shut the door. Paula stepped through, and then shut the door very quietly behind her. She waited until the other two had reached the top of the flight of stairs at the end of the passage, and then moved forward.

On the left she noticed the doorway that led to the shop. She took the staircase and paused at the top while Bridget, still talking excitedly to the doctor and without once looking back, led him up another flight of stairs to the landing above.

Paula waited again until she was sure that they had gone into a room. Through half-open doors on this first landing, she recognized the kitchen and the room where they had had breakfast. Another door looked as if it led to a bathroom. Bridget's bedroom must be on the floor above.

In Bridget's cupboard, Zavvy had said. A dark blue canvas hold-all.

Quickly and silently Paula ran up the next flight of stairs. Nicholas's bedroom must be the one at the front of the building. The door was closed but she could hear their voices, all three of them talking at once. Bridget sounded shriller than ever, the doctor was obviously trying to make himself heard, and drowning them both out was the old man's shouting.

"He ran me down! He could have killed me!"

"There's no very serious damage done," said the doctor, "but we'll have to X-ray that leg."

"I won't go to hospital!" shouted Nicholas Wild. "I want that fellow prosecuted!"

Bridget intervened. "But we don't know who he is—you didn't get the registration number."

"I know who he is, the sneaky bastard."

Paula, who had now reached the upper landing, was so fascinated by what she was hearing that she was almost tempted to stay and listen a little longer, but when she heard the doctor say he would have to call an ambulance, she knew there was no time to waste.

The door of the other room, which must be Bridget's, was ajar. The room was small and overcrowded but comparatively tidy. The "cupboard" was a big, old-fashioned wardrobe, crammed with clothes, books, shoes, some old handbags, and many other items. From a shelf at the top Paula dragged down a very shabby blue canvas bag closed by a zip-fastener. It was bulky but not excessively heavy. Taking care not to let it bump against the wall or the banisters, she crept down the two flights of stairs and along the dark passage to the outer door.

She had just reached it when she heard Bridget's high voice: "Who's that? I'm sure I heard somebody there."

The doctor's voice answered. "You had a visitor. She came in with me. Perhaps she's got tired of waiting."

Paula hurried out of the house and ran to her car. She had achieved her objective. It was almost too good to be true, and finding out what had happened to Nicholas, curious though she was, would have to wait until later. She flung the canvas bag onto the passenger seat and drove hastily away. As far as she could tell, nobody from Nicholas's place had actually seen her leave. The doctor had seen her and spoken to her, of course; no doubt he was going to be hotly questioned by Bridget and by Nicholas too, if his mind could be diverted from his own grievances.

This did not worry Paula unduly. She did not for a moment suppose that the doctor would want to be involved with his difficult patient for any longer than was necessary. He would not be interested in Paula either. He would simply reply that the visitor must have decided to go, and that was that.

More worrisome was that Bridget might discover the loss of the canvas bag. Paula had quickly pushed the other items on the shelf around so that there was not too obvious a gap, and at the moment Bridget was very much occupied with her grandfather. With luck she would not notice anything just yet, and if and when she did, decided Paula, Zavvy would have to sort it out.

She had driven away from the greengrocer's shop in the easiest direction, intent only on escaping unseen, but now she found herself in the next road to Barley Avenue. The longing to open the bag and examine its contents could not be held back any longer. She drove to the end of the road—it was a cul-de-sac—and parked in front of a huge mansion that looked as deserted as the house next door to the Macgregors.

Nobody was in sight. There was no reason she should not stay here in her car for as long as she liked, and it was nobody else's business to watch what she was doing. Nevertheless Paula found herself glancing nervously around as she tugged at the zip-fastener, almost convincing herself that somebody had followed her; that Kevin Casey, who had a habit of turning up unexpectedly, would suddenly appear at the window of her car to watch her search for the hidden treasure.

The bag was opened at last and Paula tugged at the contents. There were shirts and jeans and socks, a small radio, a little traveling chess set; and paperback books that normally Paula would have looked at with interest as a clue to their owner's tastes, but that now she simply noted as being mostly connected with the theater as she put them aside.

Underneath them was an item that caused her to believe at first that she had found the prize. It was a big envelope containing a black folder that held many sheets of manuscript. Holding her breath, Paula opened the folder and studied the top page.

The first thing that struck her was that this was not G.E. Goff's handwriting. He had always written the first draft of his novels by hand, right up to the very last. That she knew, and she also knew his writing well from her own research.

This writing was very different. It wasn't small and disciplined, but sprawling and uncertain, with many crossings-out and insertions. The manuscript was untitled, but as she examined it further she found that it was not the beginning of a novel at all; it was a lengthy introduction, in the manner of George Bernard Shaw, to what looked as if it was going to turn into a stage play.

This could surely have nothing to do with G.E. Goff. Her disappointment was acute, but short-lived. Something in her had not really expected to find the hidden treasure. It had all been too easy. If it existed at all, it would not be retrieved in this manner.

Unless—and this was a possibility, though a remote one—unless G.E. Goff had in his youth once started to write a play and had dictated it to somebody else. To his sister maybe?

Paula began to flick through the manuscript pages. It would be of interest to scholars, of course, but of no very great financial significance, if this could be proved to be the work of G.E. Goff. Perhaps Aunt Isobel didn't realize this. Perhaps she believed that anything written by her brother would command a very high price.

This handwriting. Had she seen anything similar during her own researches? Could it possibly be Aunt Isobel's own handwriting?

The answer to the first question was no, and the second question could not be answered, since Paula had never seen a sample of Aunt Isobel's writing.

Suppose it was nothing at all to do with Isobel Macgregor (née Goff). The bag itself was Zavvy's, and it was obviously of importance to him or he wouldn't have asked Paula to get it back from Bridget. There was no reason it should contain anything of Aunt Isobel's. It was Paula herself who had made the connection because Aunt Isobel had said that she had given it to Zavvy to take care of.

Assuming that the bag's contents were purely personal to Zavvy, could the play be his own work?

This was a far more likely hypothesis, given his interest in the theater and his undoubted ability as an actor.

Paula began to study the script more closely. It had a historical theme. A young woman at the time of Shakespeare wanted to write a play. Her parents, her lover, her brother, her sister, and everybody else was trying to persuade her that she could not possibly do such a thing.

The writing was very uneven. Some of the dialogue was very stilted, some of it was really convincing, and occasionally even moving. Could a young man like Xavier possibly have written it? It had a genuine ring of the period; it was unmistakably sympathetic to the young woman's point of view.

It didn't seem like the work of Zavvy as she knew him, but then she really did not know him at all. There was no reason why a play or a novel sympathetic to women should not be written by a male author. Many examples instantly sprang to mind. Shakespeare himself, Tolstoy, Flaubert, George Meredith . . . the list was endless.

Even G.E. Goff himself. Nobody who judged him only from his novels would imagine that he could be so bitterly unfriendly to women in his own private life.

At this point in her train of thought Paula suddenly exclaimed aloud, "This is hopeless. I'm getting nowhere and I'm wasting a lot of time."

Hastily she assembled the sheets of manuscript and put them back in the folder and replaced it in the envelope. Then she ruffled through the rest of the contents of Zavvy's bag to make sure that she had not missed anything of importance, repacked it, closed the zip, and dumped the bag back onto the passenger seat.

Disappointment had given way to a fresh curiosity. Who was the author of this manuscript? Well, she would soon learn that from Zavvy, she thought, as she drove up to the end of the cul-de-sac, turned the car round, and came slowly back to Barley Avenue.

She had been gone for about an hour and a half, but it seemed even longer. James must have been worrying about her. Suddenly she was terribly impatient to reassure him and to tell him what she had discovered.

The police car was gone, of course, and she could see no sign of Dr. Broadbent's Volvo, nor of the small Ford that Kevin was driving. That pleased her but did not entirely surprise her, for she had a strong suspicion that it was Kevin who had tried to run down Nicholas Wild and actually caused him quite a nasty injury.

If she was right in this, then Kevin would have disappeared, at least for the time being. That would be a great comfort.

Paula pulled up under one of the chestnut trees opposite the Macgregors' house. It all looked very peaceful and respectable, just as it had looked when she and James had first arrived.

More and more impatient to be with him, she pulled the canvas bag out of the car and hurried up to the gate. It was only then that she noticed that James's car, too, was missing.

Disappointed but not, at that moment, seriously worried, she came slowly up the steps to the front door. She remembered that she had no key and paused for a moment. If neither James nor Kevin was there, who would be at home? Just the old couple, presumably.

Paula did not want to disturb Aunt Isobel, but she had no choice but to ring the bell. Uncle Mac would have to come to the door. This was not a comfortable thought, for she was afraid that his ill will towards James and herself was beyond cure.

Feeling nervous, she touched the bell. Even if Uncle Mac won't let me in, she told herself, surely he must tell me what is going on, where James has gone, and whether he has left any message for me.

After waiting some time she rang the bell again. There must be somebody at home. Uncle Mac would not have gone out and left Aunt Isobel alone. Perhaps he had looked out of a window and seen Paula and decided not to come to the door. Or perhaps Aunt Isobel had been taken very ill and they had all gone to the hospital with her.

Paula rang the bell a third time, holding her finger down firmly and making quite sure that she could hear it ring. If nobody comes, she decided, she would go round to the back of the house and see if there was any way of getting in. Or if there was anybody out in the garden or in the summer house.

Neither of these possibilities seemed likely. All things being equal, one would expect people to be sitting in their gardens on such a fine summer day, but the Macgregor household was too much occupied with other matters.

I must do something, though, she said to herself as she picked up the canvas bag and started to walk round the side of the house.

14

Outside the back door Paula put down the canvas bag for a moment. It was beginning to feel very heavy, but she could not bear to let it out of her sight. Even if it did not contain a valuable manuscript, it still held a clue, she felt sure of that.

Then she looked down the garden towards the summer house. It all looked very peaceful, but there was no sign of human life. For a moment she felt tempted to walk over to the garden chair on the shady side of the lawn and rest there, looking at the roses and listening to the birds and the bees, until somebody came home. If it hadn't been for the summons by James's aunt, Paula thought, this was what they would both have been doing this very moment in their own garden. It was rare for the English weather to be so kind; it was silly not to take advantage of it.

Reluctantly she picked up the canvas bag again and stepped towards the back door. It opened, and she said to herself, Uncle Mac is at home then. Either he is resting and does not want to be disturbed, or else he does not want to let me in.

She crossed the little scullery and went into the kitchen. Everything looked very clean and tidy. Kevin Casey is certainly a blackmailer and probably a lot of other things as well, she thought, but he is also a very conscientious domestic worker. Once again she put down the canvas bag, fetched herself some orange juice from the fridge, and sat down to drink it.

The feeling of alarm that had hit her while she waited on the front doorstep had now passed, but she was still uneasy. Was old Mr. Macgregor somewhere upstairs, sleeping or sulking? Or was she alone in this strange house? And if so, why were they all gone and why had the back door been left unlocked?

If Aunt Isobel had been rushed to hospital, surely James, at least, would have made sure the house was locked up.

To rest and wait patiently in the garden, which a few moments ago had seemed so attractive, now seemed impossible.

Paula picked up the canvas bag and went slowly upstairs. The house was completely silent except for the ticking of the grandfather clock on the landing.

She checked the room that she and James were occupying. His hairbrush and a few other items that she had fetched for him from home were still there, and this brought a little reassurance. James, at least, would be coming back, and she only wished it could be very soon.

Meanwhile she would have to find out whether anybody else was at home. She put Zavvy's old bag down on the floor, suddenly feeling that she could not bear to tote it around any longer. It seemed to have lost its magic. The mystery of the empty house had taken over from the mystery of the missing manuscript, at least for the time being.

The door of Aunt Isobel's room was slightly ajar. That means there's nobody there, thought Paula, and she was right. The bed was made up, but not particularly neatly; one of the wardrobe doors had been left open, and one of the cushions on the big green armchair had slipped to the floor.

Kevin hasn't been in here, was Paula's first thought. This looks more like James, or perhaps Uncle Mac. At least it bore out the theory that Aunt Isobel had been taken to the hospital, and that they had all gone off in a hurry.

I'll phone Dr. Broadbent, she decided. She probably won't be there, but somebody will know about the emergency. So confident was Paula that this was the explanation for the empty house that she almost abandoned her search. But the door next to Aunt Isobel's was also ajar, and it seemed sensible to make sure that Uncle Mac was not in the house before she started telephoning.

She knocked on the door of the room. There was no response. Feeling nervous and rather guilty, she pushed the door open. The bed was opposite to her, alongside the window. On the bed lay the old man, fully dressed and fast asleep.

Paula's first feelings were almost more of annoyance than of shocked surprise. This made nonsense of her theory. How could he be lying here fast asleep when his wife was so critically ill? Even if he didn't care about her, even if he actually wished her dead, he would still put on a suitably concerned act in front of the doctor and James.

I'm going to wake him, said Paula to herself. It's not really my business, but all the same I am going to wake him.

"Mr. Macgregor!" she called loudly.

There was no response. She took a step nearer and for the first time noticed something odd about the way he was lying.

He was on his back, propped up against a rise of pillows. That was natural enough. He might have breathing problems and feel better in this position. But people thus resting surely did not normally hold their arms so stiffly by their sides. And, even more remarkable, they didn't usually lie down to rest with their shoes on.

A heart attack? A stroke?

In all their worry about Aunt Isobel, it had never once occurred to either James or herself to wonder about Uncle Mac's state of health.

Paula came close to the bed and bent over him.

"Mr. Macgregor!"

She spoke not loudly, but very clearly, and again there was not the slightest response.

She stretched out a hand and felt his wrist. There seemed to be no pulse. She straightened up again and looked around the room. On the shelf over the washbasin was a small shaving mirror. She fetched it and held it in front of the slightly open mouth for a few moments. When she removed it and looked at the glass she could see no sign of clouding. The mirror remained clear, and there was no sign that he was breathing.

"He's dead," she said aloud, putting the mirror down on the bedside table. "What ought I to do?"

The answer was obvious. There was nothing she could do except call a doctor at once.

She ran downstairs to the sitting room and found the list of phone numbers.

A woman's voice answered from Dr. Rose Broadbent's office. "I can't contact Dr. Broadbent," she said in response to Paula's request, "but I'll try to get one of the other partners. Hold on."

She did not keep Paula waiting for long.

"Dr. Cooke will be with you as soon as possible. Within the next ten or fifteen minutes, with luck. Don't touch anything. Okay?"

Paula thanked her, replaced the phone and then, feeling suddenly weak, sat down and closed her eyes.

Ten or fifteen minutes. Don't touch anything.

But I must go and have another look at that room, she said to herself, before the doctor comes. It's my only chance.

Slowly, still feeling a sense of shock, she made her way upstairs again and stood looking round Uncle Mac's room.

It was comfortable enough but not luxurious. There was a small armchair, a large built-in clothes closet, and some shelves containing books and journals. Just above the washbasin was a large wall cupboard, which was locked.

Medicines, drugs, thought Paula. He used to have a chemist's shop. Somebody had mentioned that he had kept a lot of his stock when he finally retired.

Drugs combined with alcohol. A deadly cocktail. That must surely be the answer. But had he mixed it himself or had somebody else contrived it?

Paula walked over to the window, avoiding looking at the bed. One of the window curtains was partially drawn across, presumably to cut out the brightness of the afternoon sun. Forgetting for the moment that she was not meant to touch, Paula automatically pulled it back and looked out to see if there was any sign of the doctor arriving.

The street was as quiet as ever.

I don't know what I'm looking for, thought Paula, and I don't feel at all well.

She turned to leave the room, and as she did so, she caught sight of a long white envelope lying on the window-sill. There was a handwritten name and address on it, and Paula bent over to read.

"For the attention of Mr. G. Nicholson, Nicholson and Birmingham, Solicitors."

There followed an address in a street in the neighborhood of the Law Courts in the Strand.

Mr. Macgregor had very recently written to his solicitors and now he was dead. What was in that letter? A will, was

Paula's first guess; or at any rate, some instructions about a will.

And now he was dead. How and why? Who would benefit by his death? Had somebody killed him? In that case, why had they not removed the letter?

Perhaps it had nothing to do with it. Or perhaps it was a suicide note. A very odd one and a very long one, thought Paula, and surely it is most unusual for somebody to address a suicide note to a solicitor. But then, the whole business was very odd, and it must have happened after all the others had left the house.

Unless, unless . . .

Paula stood looking at the long white envelope addressed to the firm of lawyers. The urge to open it and read the contents was gnawing at her. "I mustn't, I mustn't," she said aloud, clasping her hands tightly together. "The doctor will be here at any moment. If only I'd got time, I could steam it open . . ."

She was released from this torment of temptation by the sound of the doorbell. She ran down, opened the door, took one look at the man standing there, and exclaimed, "You're Dr. Cooke? How extraordinary. We met on Mr. Wild's doorstep."

"And you are—?" he said.

She gave her name and added, "Mrs. Macgregor is my partner's aunt. We've both been staying here. I don't know where James and his aunt have got to, but it's her husband who is dead upstairs."

They started up the stairs, Paula leading the way.

"What happened to Mr. Wild?" she asked. "Or aren't you supposed to talk about your patients?"

"He refused to go to hospital. I've sent a nurse in to dress his leg," replied Dr. Cooke.

"Poor Bridget. I didn't stay because I didn't think she'd want a visitor just then."

At the top of the stairs they paused for a moment and Paula said, "What a coincidence, you coming here."

"Not particularly," he replied placidly. "I'm working as a locum in the same practice as Dr. Broadbent. There are six partners in the practice, and a lot of people living in this locality are registered there."

"Including Mr. Wild. No, I suppose it's not such a coincidence after all. Do you know Dr. Broadbent?"

"Only very slightly. I only started last week. Now I think I'd better take a look at Mr. Macgregor."

"Of course." Paula pushed open the door of the room and waited without speaking while Dr. Cooke examined the dead man."

"You've not touched anything?" he then said.

"Only the mirror to check the breath. Otherwise it's just as I found it when I came in about twenty minutes ago."

"And the next of kin?"

"His wife. James's aunt. I've no idea where they are. Dr. Broadbent was here earlier today to see Mrs. Macgregor, who has had several heart attacks. James wanted her to go to a nursing home, and all I can suppose is that that's where they are. Unless she became worse and was taken to the hospital. But I can't find any message left for me. I just don't know what's happening at all."

Paula was conscious of the note of desperation in her own voice as she said these last words.

Dr. Cooke glanced at her and then said in his calm and unhurried manner, "You've had a bit of a shock, Professor Glenning. And I'm having a very busy afternoon. Is there somewhere we can make tea while we decide what to do?"

Paula nodded and led the way to the kitchen.

The hot sweet liquid was surprisingly comforting. She lit

a cigarette, offered one to the doctor, and was surprised when he accepted it.

"Sinners, aren't we," he said with a smile. "But there are many worse things than nicotine. It's a question of moderation in all things, and a little common sense. Did Mr. Macgregor smoke, do you know?"

"I don't know," Paula replied. "I hardly know him."

"Drink much?"

"I couldn't help noticing the glass. And the smell. They seem to consume a fair quantity of whisky in this house. How did he die, Dr. Cooke?"

"I don't know. I'm afraid I can't give a death certificate and there will have to be an autopsy."

"Drink and drugs?" suggested Paula.

"That's my guess, but what sort and how much, and why . . . I haven't the slightest idea without further investigation."

"And I can't give you any help. Actually I did wonder, when I found him. I mean, I did look around for an empty bottle or something similar. He was a chemist, I do know that, and I believe he has quite a cupboard full of medicines."

"Locked up," said Dr. Cooke. "At least he doesn't appear to have been irresponsible. Now what I am going to do, if you will lead me to a telephone, is try to track down Dr. Broadbent, because this is certainly her business."

"And if we could find out where James and Mrs. Macgregor have got to," said Paula as they moved into the sitting room, "it would help a lot."

"Have you phoned your own home?"

"Not yet. I really don't know why. I think I must have been in some sort of shock when I found him," replied Paula, omitting to say that at that moment she had been even more eager to satisfy her own curiosity than to get in touch with James. "You do your call first," she added. "That's the most important."

Dr. Cooke was examining the list of numbers. "If I can't get her," he said, "then I'll have to call the police."

"Damn," said Paula. "Yes, I suppose so. I suppose it could be—"

"Foul play, as they say in the old-time detective stories. Maybe, but it's hard to believe that an experienced pharmacist could be inveigled into swallowing a lethal dose of anything."

"He might have taken it himself."

"Indeed he might."

"Did you notice the letter to his solicitors?"

"Yes. Now let's get to work."

15

"Dr. Broadbent has just left," said Dr. Cooke ten minutes later. "Yet again. I'm going to give up. Would you like to try your home once more before I call the police?"

"I might as well, I suppose," said Paula dejectedly. She reached for the phone, and at that very moment it rang.

"Yes," she said wearily, but a second later she completely came to life again.

"Zavvy! Where are you?"

"At your place, just got in. We were trying for ages to get hold of you. James wants you to know that he's on his way."

"He's been back home? What happened? Where's Mrs. Macgregor?"

"She's in St. Mary's Nursing Home, here in Hampstead," he replied, rather too slowly for Paula's impatience. "James brought her there. She's not to have any visitors or phone calls."

"But is she ill, really badly ill?" cried Paula.

"I guess it's more a precautionary measure," said Xavier, still speaking very carefully.

"But why? What happened? Oh do hurry up, Zavvy!"

"I don't really know, but James will tell you when he gets back. He's on his way now and he ought to be with you in twenty minutes or so. What's the matter, Paula? You sound a bit—"

He broke off, searching for the appropriate word for the role he was now playing.

"What is the matter," she said crisply, "is that when I got back here I found Mr. Macgregor dead, and the doctor who is with me now can't give a death certificate, and he's going to call the police in a minute, and he urgently needs to speak to Mr. Macgregor's next of kin."

"Oh." Zavvy was momentarily speechless before he reverted to his normal self. "What a bloody awful thing for you to find. I'm sorry, Paula. What was it? Did somebody knock him on the head like my poor old Ma?"

"No, but it certainly wasn't natural," she replied grimly. "I'd better get off the phone and leave it to the doctor."

"Sorry, Paula," he said again. "Is there anything I can do?"

"Just look after our house," she said, "and the cats. Are they all right?"

The thought of Sally and Sam brought a wave of longing to be back in her own home.

"They're climbing over me now," said Zavvy. "Oh shit! Sam's just stuck a claw into my hair. Hi, Paula, don't ring off—that old bag of mine—did you ask Bridget?"

"I've got it. We'll bring it to you as soon as we can get away."

"Thanks a lot. See you."

Paula put the phone down, vastly relieved to know that James would soon be arriving, but also a little concerned that Zavvy might take it into his head to telephone Bridget. If she could tell him her story first, she felt sure he would be amused, but if Bridget were to tell the tale it could sound very different. She comforted herself with the thought that Bridget would be so occupied with her grandfather that she would have no thought for anything else, at least for the time being.

Meanwhile Dr. Cooke had finished his phone call to the police. "Inspector Martin," he said, "who I gather is investigating another recent death at this address, would very much like to speak to—er—"

"James Goff," said Paula hastily. "He's a colleague of mine at the Princess Elizabeth College. I've just been told that he's taken his aunt—Mr. Macgregor's wife—to a nursing home near our house, and that he's on his way back here and will be arriving any moment now."

"Good. We're to call Inspector Martin as soon as he arrives. This seems to be rather an unlucky household. What was this other death? Any connection?"

Paula explained, sticking to the facts and omitting her own suspicions.

"It sounds to me as if somebody did attack the housekeeper," commented Dr. Cooke when she had finished. "Probably on the spur of the moment, not with forethought. Any sign of the 'blunt instrument' beloved of detective story writers?"

"None at all, as far as I know," replied Paula. "I rather think it was just somebody's fist."

"Any reason why?"

"None that I have heard of. James and I had only just met her for the first time. I must admit that we found her an extremely irritating woman, but that's hardly a reason to kill somebody or even to hit them."

"Maybe not," said the doctor, "but then, how many people are governed by reason? Very few, I suspect."

"I wonder if Nicholas Wild is ruled by reason," said Paula thoughtfully.

"Certainly not, from what I saw of him, but then, few people are when they've had a shock and are in pain."

Paula felt sufficiently encouraged by this response to make further inquiries. She was feeling quite at ease now with this calm and friendly stranger, and it was a relief to talk to somebody who was not personally connected with the Macgregors' affairs.

"James and I are rather suspicious of Nicholas Wild," she said. "Why is somebody, living in a very modest way over his shop, in a position to buy the next door house to this one?"

"Is he?"

Paula explained. Dr. Cooke, for all his air of detachment, was not averse to a bit of gossip to pass the time of waiting, but apart from remarking that it was surprising how often seemingly poor people turned out to be very rich indeed, he had nothing much to contribute.

"It's odd, though," he added, "that he refused to go to the hospital. When people do that, it usually means they're frightened, but he didn't strike me as being fearful."

"Do you think somebody really did try to run him down?"

"It looks like it. He didn't strike me as being in the least bit paranoid either, and the granddaughter certainly believed it."

"Did she know who it was?"

"It seems not, but he certainly did know, although he didn't want to mention a name."

"That sounds suspicious," commented Paula.

"It does indeed," agreed Dr. Cooke, "but it's not my business to investigate. Two police matters in an afternoon's locum work really would be excessive."

Paula commiserated with him. "I'm afraid this Macgregor business does look as if it could be rather complicated," she added, getting up from her chair and walking over to the window. "Ah—here's James. He's going to want some tea.

I'll leave you to tell him about Mr. Macgregor. I'll be in the kitchen."

She heard James call out "Paula!" as soon as he entered the house, but she did not respond. Dr. Cooke must have come out into the hall, because she could hear him introducing himself. I'm a coward, she said to herself as she searched for the China tea that James liked so much, but I just can't face listening to his shock over Uncle Mac's death. He's going to blame himself and be upset, whereas I really don't care. They're his folks, not mine. We'll talk later, when we both feel a bit calmer.

What a blessing is Dr. Cooke, she told herself as she switched on the kettle; how lucky that it was not Dr. Broadbent who came.

But thinking it over a few minutes later, she revised this judgment. Curiosity was once again taking over from revulsion at the whole business. Dr. Broadbent would not have been so calmly impersonal; suddenly confronted with Mr. Macgregor's death, she surely would have revealed something of her own involvement, of her own feelings.

Paula picked up the tray, and found the others in the hall, just about to go upstairs. James looked as tense and worried as she had expected him to be, and he remained behind for a moment while Dr. Cooke went ahead.

"How's Aunt Isobel?" asked Paula, before James could speak.

"Fine, or rather, as well as can be expected," he replied. "She's at St. Mary's. I'm sure they'll look after her."

"I'm sure they will. And I'm on the track of something that might explain why she's been so anxious. Tell you later."

"Paula, I'm so *sorry*," he said, looking at her appealingly.

"We'll go out to dinner," she said, smiling at him, "if we

can get this business cleared up in time. There must be somewhere near here that's possible."

"Then you don't mind if we don't get home tonight?"

"No more than you do. Don't be long upstairs. The tea will get cold."

But James's tea got very cold, because almost immediately after he had gone upstairs, Inspector Martin arrived. Paula answered a few questions, and said, "Do you want me to come upstairs?"

She hoped he would say no, for she felt a very great reluctance to go into that room again and see the old man lying there.

"I don't think that will be necessary," replied Inspector Martin.

"Then I'm going in the garden. It's a lovely evening."

"You do that," he said.

He's not unlike Dr. Cooke, she thought as she came out onto the lawn. Middle-aged, world-weary, just doing his job. It was restful to be with them, but no doubt they were very different in their own homes, for it must come out somewhere, the reaction to all they saw and heard during the course of their work.

The garden felt restful too. The whole place, house and garden alike, felt empty and somehow cleansed, in spite of the fact that three men were conferring over a dead body in a little room upstairs.

Paula strolled towards the far end of the lawn, stopping for a moment by the rhododendron bush behind which she had hidden the previous night. There was no sense of apprehension now. Nicholas Wild was injured and helpless. Kevin, she felt sure, would not return to this house just yet, if at all. He must have been the driver who attacked Nicholas, and he might or might not have had something to do with Mr. Macgregor's death.

A blackmail threat repeated once too often could result in the suicide of the victim. Kevin was a blackmailer, but he was surely also a victim. Nicholas Wild had a hold over him and used it to make Kevin do what he wanted.

The pattern that lay behind the events of the last few days was beginning to take shape in Paula's mind. Nicholas, Kevin, Verena, Dr. Broadbent, and Uncle Mac—they had all been involved in some way or another. Probably not all together, in any definite conspiracy apart from Nicholas and Kevin, but all of them had been engaged in cheating Aunt Isobel, taking advantage of her frailty, making her out to be senile and incompetent with the aim of getting hold of her wealth, or potential wealth in the case of the manuscript.

Was Zavvy in it too? Paula had hoped he was not, but felt it was too early to rule him out. Bridget, she felt sure, was both ignorant and innocent of any conspiracy.

By this time Paula had reached the summer house, and she tried the glass door, not because she expected to make any fresh discovery there but because she was feeling hungry, and remembered that there was a good supply of biscuits kept in the little kitchen, among other items of refreshment.

Mildly disappointed, though not surprised, to find the door locked, she continued her wanderings, and found the beech tree where she had taken refuge while listening to Nicholas and Kevin. Beyond it was the gap in the hedge.

Even in the evening sunshine there was still a vaguely sinister feeling about the deserted garden next door, and when a white cat—surely the same one?—suddenly appeared and wound itself round her ankles, she was disproportionately startled.

Recovering herself, she bent to stroke it. "Where are you living, what have you seen, what do you know?" she murmured. "If only you could talk."

The white cat purred, and then vanished into the bushes as suddenly as it had materialized.

Paula continued along the path where she had walked the previous night, clinging to Zavvy's arm.

No wonder it had been so dark. The garden was like a jungle. Nobody had done any work here for years. But there was no sense of a story with a happy ending, only a feeling of oppression, even in the daylight, and it was a relief to come out onto what was still recognizable as the lawn, an open patch of long grass full of dandelions and plantains. From here she could at last see the back of the house.

This was particularly messy and depressing, as the backs of these huge nineteenth-century villas so often were. The stark red brick was crisscrossed with drainpipes, and the glass of the conservatory built on at one side was all of it filthy and much of it broken. Alongside was a ramshackle shed, equally disintegrating, and beyond that was the back entrance to the house.

This was locked. After attempting unsuccessfully to see something of the inside through a very dirty window, Paula moved on and came round the side of the house into the front garden, which had attracted her with its tangle of rose bushes run wild.

She was looking at them dreamily, reluctant to return to the reality of the Macgregors' house, when she saw a man with a briefcase in his hand come out of the front door and down the steps.

He looked familiar, but for the moment she could not place him. Then she remembered.

"Mr. Parkinson, isn't it," she said, coming forward. "You were here with Mr. Wild this afternoon. And you like *The Secret Garden*."

"I left some papers behind," he explained, "and as I had

another client to visit in this area I decided to collect them now."

"You work late," commented Paula.

"Any hour of the day or night," replied the estate agent, "if there's a chance of a sale. The market is dead, as no doubt you know."

"But you made a sale this afternoon. You must be very glad to get this place off your hands."

"Maybe. Maybe not. There's many a slip."

"You don't think Mr. Wild really intends to buy?"

"I can't speak for his intentions. It's his money that interests me."

"Is that doubtful?"

"It's always doubtful." Mr. Parkinson spoke as one who has seen a great deal of human nature and has no illusions about it.

"The land itself must be worth a lot," remarked Paula, hoping to learn more about Nicholas but not wanting to sound too eager. "You could get rid of this mausoleum and build half a dozen houses here."

"You're telling me," said Mr. Parkinson. "But there's no hope at the moment. No planning permission."

"Is Mr. Wild your only hope of a sale?"

"That's right."

"Then good luck to you," said Paula. "Actually I know him slightly. He's an artist, and there's plenty of room here for a studio. He might be genuine in that respect."

"An artist? He told me he had a shop."

"That too," said Paula.

They were walking together towards the gate. Paula's hopes of learning something more about Nicholas were fading. It looked as if Mr. Parkinson knew even less than she did herself.

"You know him," he said. "Do you think one can rely on him?"

"Financially, you mean? I'd guess that he is much wealthier than he appears to be."

Mr. Parkinson smiled. "But best not inquire too closely into the source of his riches," he said. "That's often the case."

They reached the front gate.

"Well, goodbye, Mrs.—er—"

Paula gave her name.

"Goodbye, Professor. I'm sorry I can't interest you in a property, but you have my card."

"Mr. Parkinson," said Paula, reluctant to let him go. "You must think me very inquisitive. Twice you've caught me looking at this house. I've a confession to make. There's a lot of disturbing things going on next door, where I'm staying at the moment, and somehow I thought Mr. Wild's purchase of this house might give a clue. Please may I ask you some questions?"

"Sure, go ahead. I'm in no hurry. I've no home life. My wife's just walked out on me. No need to commiserate. It's been on the cards for a long time. In fact, it's a relief."

"Thanks," said Paula. "Broadbent. Is that any connection with Dr. Rose Broadbent, who is a doctor practicing in this locality?"

"Not that I know of. Sounds unlikely to me. Stephen Broadbent must be ninety if he's a day. No surviving children or grandchildren. Lives down on the South Coast somewhere with a dozen cats and one manservant. So they say."

"Thanks. Back to Nicholas Wild then. When you showed him round, was there anything that struck you as odd, that you wouldn't expect in a prospective buyer?"

"There's nothing you wouldn't expect in a prospective

buyer," replied Mr. Parkinson gloomily. "The things they say and do—it makes you despair of the human race. Odd? Well, I suppose the fact that he didn't seem the least bit interested in the possibilities of the property. With a place this size most people like to show off their lifestyle. 'We can build the swimming pool over there, the grand piano will fit nicely into this alcove.' You know the sort of thing."

Paula murmured her assent.

"I just assumed," went on the estate agent, "that Mr. Wild only wanted the land, that he knew something about the planning permission that we didn't, and that he was prepared to wait until he could develop it."

"I see," said Paula.

She did not add her own supposition, that Nicholas Wild had no intention of buying, but simply wanted a good excuse for being found on the premises in order to keep watch on what was happening next door.

"Well, good luck to you," she said as they reached the gate.

"Good luck to *you*," he replied. "Cheers."

16

Paula walked thoughtfully back to the Macgregors' house. The police car had gone and she could see no sign of the old Rover that Dr. Cooke had been driving. James opened the front door as she came up the steps.

"Saw you coming," he said. "Anything to report?"

He sounded weary but calm, just as she felt herself. This was a comfort.

"Not very much," she said. "Just a little bit of extra information. Have they all gone?"

"Yes, thank God, and poor old Uncle Mac as well. They'll start cutting him up as soon as possible."

"What's your guess?" asked Paula as they came into the sitting room.

"I'm not going to make one until I've had a look at this."

James produced the envelope addressed to Uncle Mac's solicitors.

"You've got it!" exclaimed Paula excitedly. "I thought the police would have taken it."

"They didn't get a chance. I nicked it before the inspector arrived."

"What about Dr. Cooke?"

"He didn't notice me taking it. Dr. Cooke is a nice guy but he doesn't want to be involved any more than he has to."

"Then let's open it quick. Do let's."

James was searching for a paperknife in the drawer of Aunt Isobel's little walnut desk. Paula would have torn open the envelope at once. James's fussiness in small matters had always irritated her. She took a deep breath, reminded herself of all her own little habits that irritated him, and said no more until he had found what he wanted. Then they sat side by side on the sofa.

The letter to the solicitor was very short. It consisted of an instruction to hand over the enclosed to Mrs. Macgregor in the event of Mr. Macgregor's death.

"I suppose I ought to give it to Aunt Isobel," said James, staring at the envelope that was enclosed with the solicitor's letter.

"Is she fit to read it?" asked Paula.

James did not immediately reply.

"It's not very tightly sealed," said Paula. "I don't think she'd notice if you opened it carefully and stuck it up again."

"I suppose not, but it still doesn't seem right."

"It wasn't right for you to open the lawyer's letter," commented Paula.

"That's different. I'll have to deal with all their business affairs now. But this is personal."

Paula was obliged to agree. Then she waited with as much patience as she could muster while he wrestled with his conscience.

"I don't like it," he said at last, "but I really think I'd better read it. If he's played one of his dirty tricks on her, the shock could finish her off on top of the shock of hearing of his death."

Paula said nothing. Curiosity was giving way to her own

scruples about reading other people's correspondence, particularly that of people as weak as Aunt Isobel, who had already suffered much from being treated as a nonperson.

Eventually James pulled open the envelope as she had suggested. "If you don't mind," he said, "I won't hand it over to you, even though I know she likes you and trusts you. It doesn't seem quite . . ."

"Yes, I know," said Paula, leaning back in her corner of the sofa and watching his face as he read. Mostly he just looked distressed, but once or twice he muttered angrily, "The old bastard."

When he had finished he said, "You can read it if you like, Paula. There's nothing detrimental to Aunt Isobel in it, just a sniveling apology to soothe his own conscience before he goes to meet his Maker. Of course he was brought up in one of those more extreme Scottish religious sects. I'd forgotten that."

"So you're quite sure he killed himself?" said Paula.

"Aren't you?"

"Well," she said slowly. "Yes, I suppose so. I don't want to read the letter. You tell me the gist."

"He seems to have been genuinely fond of her when they married," said James, "but the money was a big attraction. She was very generous to him but he could never get enough for his gambling. Stock Exchange mostly. A year or two ago she must have got really worried about the way her capital was disappearing and she tried to stop him. The result was the plot we've more or less guessed at, to get complete control over her assets. He juggled around with her medicines and managed to produce symptoms of senility."

"Dr. Broadbent," interrupted Paula. "Didn't she suspect?"

"Apparently not. He seems to have been very clever with his drug cocktail experiments. When they broke open his cupboard just now they found notebooks which interested Dr. Cooke very much. Pity all that knowledge and ingenuity couldn't have gone into something more positive and useful than cheating his wife."

"What about the clinic?" asked Paula.

"That was Dr. Rose's idea. Maybe she was a little suspicious after all. He'd have no control over Aunt Isobel's medicines while she was in there. But it seems to have worked to his advantage, with the shock of being shut up there making poor Auntie more confused than ever, and with doctor and lawyer convinced that she would never again be capable of handling her own affairs."

"So she signed away all her rights. But it would have to be made plain to her that that was what she was doing."

"I doubt if the business was very conscientiously carried out. Reading between the lines, I'd say that's where Dr. Broadbent's conscience was stifled. Maybe Uncle Mac used his suspicions that the guy who runs the clinic—Rose's boyfriend—was doing some drug dealing."

"And the lawyer?" said Paula.

James merely shrugged.

"Probably helping himself to some of Auntie's assets too," said Paula. She added, "What about the manuscript? Does he mention it?"

"Not at all."

"How very strange."

They pondered this for a while. James looked at the letter again. "I really don't think Uncle Mac could have known," he said presently. "If he'd been trying to get hold of it he'd certainly have put it in with his confession."

"It's extraordinary," Paula said, "that she talked about it to Kevin and Verena but never to him."

James was not listening; he was frowning over the letter. "He's absolutely wallowing in his own guilt. It's perfectly revolting. No, I'm sure he never knew about the manuscript. She must have kept it to herself all these years. Probably as a little nest egg, a little security of her own that he couldn't touch."

"That makes sense, I suppose," said Paula, "but I still think it's odd that she told the people in the clinic. And Zavvy maybe, when she handed it to him for safekeeping. Oh my God, that manuscript!" cried Paula, jumping up suddenly. "I'd almost forgotten about Zavvy's old canvas bag. I hope it's still there."

She ran upstairs, with James following close behind. The bag was exactly where she had left it.

Paula collapsed onto the bed, laughing.

"I think I must be losing my wits," she said. "How could anybody possibly have taken it except you or Dr. Cooke or Inspector Martin?"

"I haven't the slightest idea what you are talking about," said James reproachfully, "and I think we'd better go and get something to eat now and try to forget this whole business for a while."

"I'm sorry," said Paula. "Of course you don't know about it. I haven't had a chance to tell you."

James groaned. "Do you know, love, I honestly don't think I want to hear. Not just at this moment."

"Okay. Over dinner maybe."

"*Not* over dinner. I want to enjoy my lasagna. There's an Italian restaurant down in the High Street."

Paula jumped up from the bed. "Shall I drive? You've had a lot of it today."

James said he would rather walk, if she didn't mind. Paula agreed, and then he said, "Come on then. What are you doing *now*?"

Paula was pulling clumsily at the zip-fastener of Zavvy's

canvas bag. It caught and refused to move further. She swore at it and tugged again and made it worse.

"Come *on*!" shouted James.

But Paula could not stop herself from trying to open the zip. The thought of leaving the manuscript that she had taken such risks to obtain was intolerable. Of course they would lock up the house, but that was not enough. Anything might happen while they were away.

"I'll just have to take the whole bag with me," she said.

James exploded. She had not realized how near the end of his patience he was, how much his nerves had been affected by the recent events. He kicked the canvas bag across the floor, out of her reach, grabbed her wrist and pulled her out of the room.

"But it's a manuscript!" yelled Paula. "It could be *the* manuscript!"

There might have been just a split second before James reacted. "Fuck the manuscript! And all his works. I don't *care*. I hated the old bugger. I don't care, I don't *care* . . ."

"But Aunt Isobel," gasped Paula as she was hurried downstairs.

"She won't need any money. I'll look after her."

Paula subsided. At this moment the prospect of being somewhere noisy and cheerful with good food and drink and no associations at all with the Macgregor household was so very appealing that if James hadn't been dragging her along she would probably have gone willingly.

But an hour later, when they were considering which of the Italian ice creams to order, and James had drunk plentifully of the house wine, Paula began to worry again.

"Did you lock up before we came out?"

"Of course I did. Not that I care. You said yourself that there was nothing important enough among their possessions to be worth stealing."

Paula said no more. There was no point in nagging James now, particularly as some part of her couldn't help but feel sympathy with him. Aunt Isobel was safe and well cared for—let's forget the rest.

The night air felt pleasantly cool when they came out of the crowded little restaurant.

"Aren't you glad we didn't bring the car?" said James.

Paula agreed.

Fifteen minutes' leisurely walking brought them back to Barley Avenue. It was well past midnight and there were no lighted windows, no sign of life at all to be seen in the quiet road.

"All old people," commented James. "In ten years time they'll all be dead and all these old houses will be pulled down and there'll be a rash of little executive-type dwellings put up."

"Mr. Parkinson," murmured Paula.

"What's that?"

Paula explained about the estate agent. James was in a mellow mood now, and didn't seem to mind talking about Uncle Mac's death and the manuscript and all the rest of it. They walked more slowly while Paula told her story.

"You're crazy," he said when she described how she had extracted Zavvy's canvas bag and then run away.

A moment later he added. "It's not impossible that Grandpa dictated something to Isobel. I believe she was inclined at one time to hero-worship her older brother."

"Not jealous of him?"

"That too, probably. One doesn't necessarily exclude the other."

"Did he ever write any plays?"

"He might have. We'll have a look when we get back. At least I can tell you if it's her handwriting."

James quickened his step. Paula did likewise. At least we're really together again, she thought.

As they approached the Macgregors' front gate something flashed past them and into the neighbouring garden.

"The white cat," said Paula. "That's the third time I've seen it."

"Third time lucky," said James cheerfully.

"I hope so."

James opened the front door. The house looked exactly as they had left it.

"You wait here," he said. "I'll go and fetch it. It's such a relief to move about the place without being spied on. I had a hell of a job getting Aunt Isobel away, but I'll tell you about that later. If you want to hear."

He was going upstairs as he spoke.

Paula, suddenly restless and a little apprehensive, waited in the hall.

James reappeared at the top of the stairs.

"Where did you actually leave it?" he called out.

Paula did not reply. She rushed upstairs and into the bedroom, quickly looked around, and then sat down.

"I knew it," she said very quietly. "I knew I ought to take it with me."

"But this is absurd." James, who had now sobered up completely, was protesting with all the vehemence of one who feels guilty but is not going to admit it. "It can't have disappeared. Are you quite sure you left it in here?"

"I left it in here," replied Paula in the same very quiet voice, "and you kicked it out of my hands. Remember?"

James made a grimace but said nothing. Paula stood up with an air of determination and said, "Who else has the keys to this house besides yourself?"

"As far as I know," replied James slowly, "only Uncle Mac and Aunt Isobel and the housekeeper."

"The housekeeper," repeated Paula. "What happened to Verena's keys after she died?"

"I don't know," said James unhappily. "Presumably Uncle Mac took charge of that."

"And how about Kevin? I suppose Uncle Mac gave him the keys to the house. And no doubt he never returned them."

James's silence was plainly an assent. He was looking very unhappy. Paula reached out and held his hand for a moment.

"The interrogation is now at an end," she said, almost cheerfully. "Don't let's do any blaming. I never thought about it either, and I've been happily convincing myself that Kevin would never risk coming back to this house after what has been happening."

"Why wouldn't he risk it?"

Paula quickly explained her reasoning. "He'd want to keep out of the way after running his car at Nicholas Wild," she concluded.

"It doesn't have to have been Kevin," said James when she had finished. "There must be plenty of people with a grudge against old Nick. Or it could even have been a genuine accident."

"I know, I know. We've both made a mess of this. All the same, I think Kevin is the most likely."

"I suppose we'd better look around the house," said James without enthusiasm, "just to check that nothing else is gone."

"If you say so," said Paula with equal reluctance."

Fifteen minutes later they met in the kitchen.

"Notice anything?" said Paula.

"No. Did you?"

"Only that Aunt Isobel's room looks as if somebody has tidied it up. That's Kevin's trademark—he simply can't see a cushion out of place without putting it back. Do we know where he lives?"

"Presumably the agency has an address."

"He'll have left it."

"You said that before. What I'm wondering is what he'll do if he finds this isn't what he's looking for, and in any case, how would he dispose of it if he did find a genuine G.E. Goff novel?"

"Nicholas would see to that," said Paula. "I'm sure he's making a business of stolen pictures, forgeries—you name it."

"But you said Kevin drove his car at Nicholas," objected James.

"And you said it might have been somebody else. Is there a phone in here?"

"On the dresser. Why d'you want it?"

"I want to see if Zavvy is at home."

"He wouldn't have the keys to this house."

"How do we know? In any case, he's very good at climbing into places," added Paula.

"There's no reply," she said after waiting for a while.

"It's very late. He's probably asleep."

Paula sighed. "I'm afraid you're right. That boy is very good at sleeping too. Oh James, if only there was something we could *do*," Paula went on, moving restlessly about the kitchen. "I'm never going to get to sleep myself. I'm feeling much too frustrated."

She wandered out into the little scullery that led to the back door, and called out, in quite a different tone of voice: "James—did you bolt the back door before we went out?"

"Of course I did. I always do."

"Well it's not bolted now. Locked but not bolted. Whoever it was must have left this way. I wonder . . ."

Paula unlocked the door and moved out onto the lawn. James followed her.

"He wouldn't want to risk being seen," she said, "even if everyone in the street was fast asleep. One never knows."

"Hi—where are you going?" called out James as she proceeded to walk further into the garden.

"Just a hunch," she called back.

"Not the summer house?"

"Not. Next door. I wish you'd come too. I hate the dark."

"Okay. Wait while I get a torch."

Together they made their way through the gap in the hedge.

"I'm sure he'd have come out this way," said Paula.

"I'm sure you're right, but I still don't see why we—"

"Ssh." She interrupted him. "What's that noise?"

They stood absolutely still in the jungle of bushes. Among the little crackling and swishing sounds of the night there was a different sound, faint but quite distinguishable as a human sound.

"I think it's straight ahead," whispered Paula.

"So do I."

"If it really is him—"

"It sounds as if he's hurt himself. Tripped or something."

They moved forward carefully. The sound of somebody groaning became louder and clearer.

James flashed the light about and finally brought it to rest on something a few feet ahead of them. Paula moved into the beam, bent over, then straightened up again.

"Kevin?" called out James.

"No." She hesitated for a moment. "Not Kevin. It's Zavvy."

17

Zavvy, having succeeded in raising himself slightly off the ground, was shifting about, groaning and swearing, and trying to free his foot, which had got entangled in an old tree stump. With the help of James and Paula he eventually managed to stand up, but he still clung to them and continued to swear.

"Can you walk?" asked James.

A careful experiment proved that he could.

"It's my head," he said, at last speaking coherently. "I was chasing him and he hit me. Hurts like hell."

"Okay. We'll get you home and have a look at it."

Paula dropped behind and let James take over.

Her first assumption had been that Zavvy was the thief, if indeed it was theft to remove one's own property. She had felt disappointed in him, and had then reminded herself that her own action had definitely been a theft. And when Zavvy had said someone else had hit him, which judging from appearances was true enough, her thought ran along quite different lines.

The inspection of Zavvy's injury resulted in a lively argument. James thought he ought to go to the hospital. Zavvy was sure that the antiseptic ointment and the plaster was all that was needed. Paula, remembering Nicholas Wild's shouting, took no part in the discussion.

"I don't feel bad now," said Zavvy quietly but firmly, after James had expressed his opinion for the third time, "and if it's delayed concussion there's no way of knowing until after the delay so I might just as well stay here meanwhile."

James found it difficult to argue with this reasoning, and Paula suspected that he was in fact just as keen as she was to listen to the boy's story.

After assuring them that he had taken all security measures before he left their house in Hampstead, and that plenty of food and water had been left for the cats, he explained that he had phoned Bridget because he thought she'd be worrying about him. She had been extremely agitated and had told him a confused story about somebody attacking her grandfather.

"And about Paula nicking a canvas bag," he added, turning to laugh at her and then wincing as the movement aggravated his headache.

"I told you on the phone that I'd got it," said Paula reproachfully.

"Sure, but I got kinda worried. I hope you don't mind me leaving your place."

They reassured him and begged him to continue. After a long journey by bus and tube train he'd arrived at Barley Avenue only about ten minutes before they found him. He'd rung the bell, and when there was no reply he'd decided that they must be fast asleep.

This was very disappointing, but since he couldn't get into the house he decided to spend the rest of the night in the summer house, as he had done on previous occasions. That was when he saw this guy snooping around the garden. Stupidly he had called out to him.

"Stop thief!" cried Zavvy with a dramatic gesture, and then added, "Ouch!" and put a hand to his head again.

"He was carrying something," he continued more quietly. "I caught up with him and tried to get it. That's when I guessed what it was. I'm not quite sure what happened next, except that I was on the ground with a hell of a headache and this bloody great light in my eyes."

"So what happened to the bag?" asked Paula.

"Didn't you chase him?" Zavvy sounded quite indignant.

"We didn't know he was there," retorted James.

"No. I guess not. Sorry." Zavvy groaned again and put his hand to his head.

"I think you'd better go to bed," said Paula, standing up.

This time Zavvy made no objection, and Paula, really concerned for him, accompanied him up to the room that had been his mother's.

At the sight of it he came to life a little.

"What happens to all this?"

"If you are her nearest surviving relative, which presumably you are," replied Paula, "then her possessions will no doubt be yours. But don't worry about it at the moment. You can talk to James about it tomorrow. There's going to be a lot of sorting out to do, particularly if Mrs. Macgregor is not able to return home at all."

Zavvy yawned again and collapsed onto the bed. Paula, who had been rigidly holding back her own curiosity up till now, could not stop herself from asking, before he fell asleep, "Zavvy, that manuscript of a play that's in your bag—is it yours?"

"Mine? How do you mean—mine?"

He sounded both suspicious and indignant. Paula reminded herself that this was the first time a manuscript had been mentioned between them. It had been Aunt Isobel who told her she had given the manuscript to Zavvy for safe-keeping.

"Did you write it?" asked Paula.

"Me? Write a play? You must be joking."

"I don't see why you shouldn't," retorted Paula with spirit. "You can play many roles, you've got a good ear for different forms of speech—so good that I never know when you're being yourself and when you're mimicking somebody. If you didn't write it, do you know who did?"

"It depends what you mean by 'know.'" Xavier was thoroughly awake again now. "I got it from Mrs. Macgregor. It seemed to be something she thought was very valuable and she was sure somebody was trying to steal it from her. She said she believed it would be safe with me. With me!—dividing my time between a squat and the summer house! Anyway, to please her I took it. I like her, as you may have noticed, and she likes me, and we both like acting."

"Did you read it?" asked Paula.

"No time," he replied shortly. "I just glanced at it, thought it looked interesting. But I was worried about where to put it. Obviously it mattered a lot to her, whether or not it was worth anything, but she didn't want it in this house and I didn't want it in the squat. The only thing I could think of was to ask Bridget to hang on to it for me."

"You didn't tell Bridget about the manuscript?"

"No. Better not. I put it in with some of my books and gear—I didn't think she'd bother to look inside."

"Do you think she did look?"

"I don't know." Zavvy groaned. Paula had the impression that this time it was only partly because of his headache. "I've never known her like this," he went on. "I've got a funny sort of a feeling that it's all over between us, as they say."

"I'm sorry," said Paula, "and I'm sorry to keep you talking when you ought to be resting. I'll leave you in peace now."

"I'm wide awake now," grumbled the boy.

Paula laughed and walked to the door, then looked back. As she had expected, he was flat out on the bed and if not already asleep, not very far from it.

"I think he's telling the truth," she said to James as she came into their room.

There was no response. James, too, was fast asleep, or at any rate pretending to be, and Paula did not dare to disturb him.

Feeling very frustrated, and convinced that there was to be no sleep for her that night, she went downstairs and made a cup of coffee and took it into the sitting room. There she settled herself comfortably in a corner of the sofa, lit a cigarette, and began to think over the events of the day.

There's a pattern forming, she said to herself as she had said earlier, and it's becoming more and more clear.

She stubbed out the cigarette end into an ashtray and contemplated reaching for another. She closed her eyes and tried to think. She found that the pattern was not becoming clearer at all, but was more and more confused. In fact it became quite fantastical, with a figure who had Zavvy's face dressed up like Macbeth and storming around a vast and empty auditorium, and herself—or was it herself?—dodging along one row of seats after another in a more and more desperate attempt to escape him.

Suddenly she sat bolt upright on the sofa, feeling dizzy and very stiff. She looked with great alarm at the ashtray on the coffee table beside her.

"I must have been asleep for hours," she said aloud. "I

could have set the house on fire. That settles it. I've got to try to give it up."

She stood up, stretched her arms out, and stamped her feet. The light she had switched on when she sat down was still burning. Still feeling confused, she looked at her watch. Half-past eight. She walked over to the window and pulled back the heavy velvet drapes. Bright sunlight dazzled her, and after blinking for a moment, she noticed that for once there was a little activity in Barley Avenue. A gas company van was parked opposite, and the postman was crossing the road towards the Macgregors' house.

Paula went to the front door and took from him a little pile of junk mail.

"Lovely weather," she said.

He seconded this observation and walked briskly away.

Paula dumped the rubbish letters onto the hall table and went to the kitchen to make coffee. After this she felt sufficiently alert to calculate that she must have been asleep for at least six hours. That's two nights running I've woken like this, she said to herself, but yesterday morning Zavvy brought me tea.

Zavvy. She must go and see how he was. She would not wake him, but later on, if his head wasn't a lot better, they really must get him examined by a doctor. Meanwhile what she needed was a shower. As James had said, it was nice to move about the house without the feeling of being spied on. She was just about to go upstairs when the front doorbell rang.

Parcel post, I suppose, she thought. Why can't they do it all at once?

Yawning, she opened the front door again and saw a girl standing there, a dark girl dressed in black trousers and a dark gray shirt. Only the face was very pale and looked pinched, weary, and unhappy.

It took Paula a second or two to recognize her, and then she said, without any warmth of welcome, "Bridget! What on earth are you doing here at this hour?"

"Have you got Zavvy here?" demanded the girl.

It dawned on Paula that, in addition to all her other emotions, Bridget Wild was extremely angry.

"He's upstairs asleep," she replied. "Somebody knocked him on the head last night."

"And whose fault's that!" screamed Bridget. "Yours, yours, you interfering old cow! If you hadn't—"

She broke off and glared at Paula. She looked for a moment as if she was going to hit her, but then she controlled herself and pushed past her towards the foot of the stairs. At the same time Zavvy appeared at the top of the flight, stared down at Bridget and Paula, and then leaned over the banister and slid down the smooth wooden rail to the bottom.

Here he straightened up, took a couple of slow, deliberate steps towards the two women, and said in the drawling tones of an old-fashioned stage police constable, "Nah then, what's all this 'ere?"

Bridget rushed forward, grabbed at him, and burst into tears. Zavvy put an arm round her, looked at Paula over Bridget's head, made a very extravagant grimace and used his free hand to grab at his own head again, and then propelled Bridget towards the sitting room.

Paula, torn between curiosity on the one hand and the strong desire for a shower and some more coffee on the other, finally decided on the latter course, and left them alone.

Ten or fifteen minutes later, feeling much more human, she decided to take some tea up to James, who was still half-asleep.

"Stay with me," he said, rousing himself. "I need comfort and company."

"Five minutes," said Paula, "then I've simply got to find out what Zavvy and Bridget are up to."

"Bridget?" echoed James in a dazed manner.

Paula didn't bother to explain, nor did James really want to know.

"We ought to get that boy to see a doctor," he said halfheartedly.

"Yes, I know. And we'll have to find out what his plans are."

"He's genuinely fond of Aunt Isobel," continued James. "He was terribly concerned about her yesterday afternoon."

"I know," said Paula again. "They enjoy shocking each other. It's the sort of rapport you sometimes get between the young and the very old."

At the end of five minutes Paula got up to go and James said he was going to have a shower.

"See you," said Paula.

They're very quiet, she said to herself as she approached the sitting room door. There she hesitated for a moment, not wanting to break in on any great reconciliation scene, and called out to Zavvy before pushing open the door.

There was nobody in the room. Could they have gone upstairs? she asked herself. Then she saw the piece of paper on the coffee table.

"Paula," read the note, "I've gone with B. There's a man come to see her grandpa and they've locked themselves in the room and are shouting at each other. He's hurt his leg and can't walk and she's sure the other guy is going to kill him. Back as soon as possible."

"Kevin!" said Paula aloud. "I hope we're not too late."

She ran upstairs, calling "James!" as she ran.

At the bathroom door she paused and continued to shout: "James—get dressed at once. We've got to get to Nicholas right away. Kevin's there and it's come to a showdown. Anything could happen!"

18

"But what are we supposed to *do*?" asked James as Paula drove rapidly along Barley Avenue and waited impatiently to join the traffic in the major road ahead.

"I don't know but I think we ought to be there," she replied. "We might be able to help—or prevent something. Zavvy could be putting himself at risk again."

"You're getting obsessed with that boy," grumbled James. "I grant you he's not as bad as he seemed at first, but I still wouldn't trust him beyond—"

"Aunt Isobel trusted him," interrupted Paula, "and you said yourself they liked each other. How is Aunt Isobel, by the way?"

"You think I've had time to phone the nursing home this morning?"

This weighty sarcasm went unanswered and they completed the short drive in silence.

"Can you see anywhere to park?" asked Paula as they approached the greengrocer's shop.

"No," snapped James, but nevertheless he did look around and suggested a very small gap opposite the shop. Paula, who to her own annoyance had never been good at these awkward maneuvers, made a couple of unsuccessful attempts to back her car into the gap before James pushed her out of the driving seat and out of the car and completed the job himself.

This improved his temper considerably, and Paula, deciding that this was not the moment to show resentment, expressed gratitude and relief. They crossed the road hand in hand, stood on the step in front of the dirty green door, and rattled the letterbox as loudly as they could.

Paula meanwhile was examining the door. "There is a bell after all," she said. "Right over here. But I don't suppose it works."

She pushed at the little button, which was so rusted and splashed with dark paint that she and Dr. Cooke had failed to notice it the day before.

Nothing happened.

"Can you hear anything?" she asked.

James, who had his head pressed up against the door, murmured, "Not really. Too much noise in the street. Let's throw something at the windows."

"You try that. I'll go on with the letterbox."

But there was no need for these efforts. The door was opened so suddenly that James, still leaning against it, almost fell into the house.

"Zavvy!" cried Paula, her worst fears realized.

There was blood running down the side of his face.

"It's okay," he said, managing a feeble grin. "Only superficial. I shall live. But the old guy may not. We thought you were the doctor. Or the ambulance. Or the police. What's happened to the emergency services?"

"They're not functioning," snapped James. "Like most other things in this bloody country nowadays. Come on. Where's a phone? I'll have a go."

He ran up the first flight of stairs and collided with a

distraught Bridget, who clung to him, crying, "Are you the doctor? The doctor?"

"No," said James, "but I'm going to get him for you."

They disappeared into the living room.

Paula, moving more slowly upstairs with Zavvy, suggested that he should attend to his own injuries right away.

"I'm all right," he repeated impatiently. "It's B.'s grandpa. We can't leave him. He's badly hurt. He's been shot."

"You mean—"

"Don't know the name. The guy I chased last night."

He hurried on up the second flight of stairs. Bridget appeared and ran after him. Paula remained behind to speak to James.

"Kevin's got a gun," she said.

"I know. Bridget told me. He shot the old man in the chest. Zavvy tried to stop him and Kevin turned on him and then got away. The ambulance is on the way. And the police. I don't think we can be any use upstairs. Better wait down in the hall. What are you doing, Paula?"

Paula was looking round the living room. "I'm wondering what happened to Zavvy's bag."

James made an exasperated noise. "He wouldn't have brought it with him. He'd be trying to do a deal with Nicholas since he couldn't handle the manuscript himself."

"I wish we could find it."

"I don't. I don't want anything more to do with it. There's someone coming now. More questions. I suppose we'll be here for hours."

He stamped off down the stairs to the street door.

Paula did not follow. She was by no means convinced that Kevin had not brought the manuscript into the house. It's of no use to him, she reasoned, without the knowledge of how to dispose of it. Nicholas has that knowledge. There's no love lost between them, but he's Kevin's only chance, and if Kevin can prove that there's money in it for both of them . . .

But he would have to produce a manuscript. Nicholas wouldn't believe it otherwise. How and why had they actually come to blows? Had the old man, convinced that Kevin had attacked him, refused to talk at all, refused even to look at the manuscript? Or had he been tempted to look and then discovered it was useless and accused Kevin of cheating him and attacked Kevin first?

In any case, Kevin must have lost his head and hit out yet again. Zavvy had tried to control him and got himself injured yet again, and Kevin had run away, his own escape being more urgent than saving the manuscript. Perhaps by then he had himself become convinced that it was worthless.

The more she thought about it, the more sure Paula became that the manuscript was still in the house. The need to see it again was becoming an obsession with her. She couldn't help but blame James for its loss, but she blamed herself even more.

Meanwhile there was intense activity in the house. The ambulance men with difficulty maneuvered the seriously wounded Nicholas downstairs. One of them, glancing at Zavvy, remarked that he had better come along to the hospital too, and Bridget, almost hysterical, was crying first over one of them and then over the other.

Paula remained in the little living room. James had taken charge, and nobody seemed to know or care where she was. After the ambulance had driven away she had a moment of alarm when she heard James and Inspector Martin talking on the landing.

"Where can we talk for a moment?" the inspector was asking.

Not in here please, prayed Paula.

"I don't know the house," James replied, "but this looks like the kitchen. Let's go in here."

Paula waited for about half a minute and then made a dash for the upper stairs and for Nicholas's room. There was no time to waste. The police inspector only needed to get the general picture from James and then he would be going all over the house.

The old man's bedroom was a shambles. That, Paula had expected. Among the tangle of stained bedclothes and shoes and old socks and twisted rugs on the floor she could see some sheets of typescript, some torn, some crumpled up. She grabbed what she could and then made her escape into Bridget's room, leaving the door ajar.

There was the sound of footsteps, and then suddenly James's voice, very near and very clear.

"Professor Glenning? She's in the house somewhere, keeping out of the way. Now the others have gone, she'll be joining us."

Paula, after a moment's alarm, silently thanked him. She waited until it seemed to her that they had gone into Nicholas's room, then pushed the rescued pages into her handbag without even glancing at them. She came quietly out of Bridget's room and knocked on the other door.

James opened it. "Oh. There you are." He scowled at her.

"Am I needed?" asked Paula innocently.

A brief consultation followed, during which Paula gave no indication of her impatience to be gone. James certainly wanted her out of the way. That was clear to Paula, if not to the police inspector. He's afraid I'll say something indiscreet, thought Paula, or something that conflicts with what he's said himself, and I'm afraid of that too, since I've no idea what James has said.

"I understand that Mr. Keeling was injured last night

while chasing an intruder," said Inspector Martin at last. "Have you any idea who was the intruder?"

"It might have been the man who came from an agency to act as temporary housekeeper," said Paula, refraining from glancing at James as she spoke. "That's only a guess. I didn't see anybody. Oh, and I ought to give you this."

She took out of her handbag the note that Zavvy had left. Luckily she had placed it in a different compartment from the typescript pages that she had retrieved from Nicholas's room.

The inspector took the note, glanced at it, and thanked her.

"We'll be talking to the boy shortly," he added. "I don't think we need keep you now, Professor. Where will you be if we want to get in touch?"

"I think I'd better go home. And someone ought to be visiting Aunt Isobel, don't you think, James?"

"I do indeed." James looked relieved. "I'll join you as soon as I can. We won't be much longer, will we, Inspector?"

Outside the house stood a police car, which was attracting attention from residents and passersby, and the little news agent's shop next door was overflowing with people. One of them, noticing Paula come out of the house, started to speak to her as she waited to cross the road, but she took no notice and walked determinedly towards her car.

I will go to see Aunt Isobel, she was thinking, but I'm going to the hospital first to talk to Zavvy because I may not get another chance for a long time.

The Casualty Wing at St. Sebastian's Hospital was an exceptionally depressing place, more than most such departments, for the hospital was doomed to closure, having been pronounced superfluous by the authorities, in spite of the fact that large numbers of patients passed through its doors every day.

Paper was peeling off the walls, the floor was very dirty, and the people waiting on the hard and often broken chairs looked helpless and wretched. The members of staff trying desperately to attend to them all looked equally so.

Paula's first two inquiries were met with blank looks, but the third attempt brought her an answer and she made her way to a corridor where she found Zavvy and Bridget sitting close together on a hard bench outside a door labeled "Treatment Room." Bridget looked pale but tolerably calm. Zavvy's face, Paula was glad to see, was clear of bloodstains and had acquired some more dressings.

He greeted her warmly and even Bridget looked less hostile than she had before.

"How is Mr. Wild?" asked Paula. "Any news?"

"They're going to operate," replied Zavvy. "The bullet went into the chest but they think he's got a chance. He's not conscious of course but B. wants to see him before the op. and they're going to call her any moment now."

"I'll wait a bit if I may," said Paula, sitting down. "James will be coming along later. He's occupied with the police at the moment."

"Do I have to see the police?" asked Bridget anxiously.

"I don't think they'll bother you much," said Paula. "Inspector Martin is very human."

At that point a nurse came to fetch Bridget, and Paula began at once: "Zavvy—what actually happened?"

"I got back with B.," he replied, "and found the bedroom door locked. She wanted me to break in but they seemed to have calmed down and were talking quietly. I could hardly hear them."

"But were there two voices?" broke in Paula.

"They were both talking," insisted Zavvy. "I sent B. off to

make us some breakfast so I could listen and look at the lock in peace. Actually it was a bolt, not a lock, and I could see that it wouldn't take much to break it."

"Did you hear anything they said?" Paula, afraid that either Bridget or the police might arrive at any moment, tried to control her impatience. She was longing to know whether Zavvy had seen or heard anything of the manuscript, but she didn't want to mention it unless he did so first.

"Not really," he replied. "Can't honestly say I was trying to. Just wondering what to do. Hoping it would all go away. Then they started shouting again—worse than ever. B. came rushing upstairs, yelling at me to do something, and that's when I broke in the door and the shooting started. So it's my fault if the old guy dies."

He said this defiantly, but he looked suddenly very young and scared. This time Paula didn't think he was acting.

"It's nobody's fault," she said firmly. "Bridget was just as much responsible as you were. More responsible in fact."

"Yeah, I guess so," said Zavvy, but he didn't sound very convinced.

Paula did her best to reassure him. She had learned nothing, but perhaps it served her right, she told herself, for thinking more about her own curiosity than about the feelings of the people concerned.

"I've got to go," she said standing up, "because James wants me to go and see Mrs. Macgregor."

"How is she?" asked Zavvy.

"Not too bad as far as I know. Do you want to send her a message?"

He managed a grin. "Nothing repeatable. Just tell her I'll get to see her as soon as I can."

"I'll do that," said Paula, standing up. "James will be here soon," she added in a final attempt to cheer him up a little.

But Zavvy wasn't listening. Bridget was coming out of the Treatment Room and Paula hurried away. At least they've got together again, she said to herself as she got into her car. Zavvy was wrong in thinking they were going to part. That was good. They were two lonely young people and they needed each other.

The thought should have been comforting. Paula nevertheless found herself sinking deeper and deeper into one of her occasional fits of melancholy as she drove out of the crumbling hospital, which had once stood so proudly and confidently as a haven for the feeble and the sick.

I ought to stop and have breakfast somewhere, she thought. I'm hungry and tired. But somehow it seemed easier to drive on than to stop. Depression took over, making a mockery of the bright summer morning. Everything looked shabby. The faces of the Saturday shoppers—people of many races and ages—all seemed to her to look sad and hopeless.

She drove carefully but listlessly, trying to shake off the fit of gloom by thinking about her house and the garden and the cats. And about Aunt Isobel.

At traffic lights in Hampstead High Street she debated whether to go straight home or to turn left for the nursing home. The longing to be at home was now overwhelming. Surely she could spare half an hour before making the visit. Of course she would telephone the nursing home the moment she got in, and if there happened to be any urgency . . .

The lights turned green at last, and Paula, having decided to drive straight on, infuriated every driver around her by suddenly changing her mind and turning to the left. The chorus of angry shouts and hootings shocked her into greater self-control, and she continued quickly in the direction of St. Mary's Nursing Home.

19

The matron, a large, worried-looking woman, was both relieved and reproachful.

"We've been telephoning for hours," she said. "Both numbers. We got no reply. Is Mr. Goff with you?"

Paula apologized. "He'll be along as soon as he possibly can. There's been a bit of a crisis and he's got held up. How is Mrs. Macgregor?"

"Very poorly indeed. At one time we feared she wouldn't rally, but she came round and is a little better now."

"May I see her?"

"She mustn't have any excitement." The matron looked at Paula doubtfully. "Mr. Goff didn't want her to have any visitors at all."

"Would you like to ask her if she would like to see me?" suggested Paula. "Or perhaps she may prefer to wait for her nephew."

"How long is he likely to be?"

"I'm sorry, but I simply don't know. It might be an hour or more. He asked me to come on ahead."

The matron continued to look uncertain. Paula waited with barely concealed impatience.

"I should be very grateful if you would tell Mrs.

Macgregor that Paula is here," she went on after the silence had lasted too long. "I think you will find that Mrs. Macgregor will want to see me. I shall certainly be very careful not to upset her in any way."

"Well, I suppose we could do that," said the matron.

Paula, scenting a weakness, was beginning to press the point when they were interrupted by the arrival of a nurse.

"Excuse me," she said to the matron, and then addressed Paula: "Are you by any chance Mrs. Goff?"

"Yes," said Paula.

"Then please would you come at once to see Mrs. Macgregor? She can see out of the window from her bed and she swore she saw your car arriving."

Paula followed her, scolding herself for allowing even this short delay, for if she had said straight away that she was James's wife no doubt she would have been admitted at once. It was such a trivial little thing that mattered so much to some other people and ought not to matter to her.

But it *does* matter to me, she thought as she followed the nurse along the corridor. I'm not James's wife and I never want to be. Why can't a middle-aged woman just be herself, whether she's a university teacher or a housekeeper or a brothel-keeper or whatever.

"Here she is." The nurse, a placid and kind-looking middle-aged woman, pushed open a door. "Ring if you need anything. Would you like some coffee?" she added, addressing Paula.

"Yes please," said Paula gratefully.

Aunt Isobel certainly seemed to be more pale and frail than ever, but there was a look in her eye that showed her mind and spirit were still very much alive.

Paula drew up a chair.

"Not there," said Aunt Isobel. "Sit where I can see you."

Paula shifted. "Is that better?"

"Yes. I thought you were never coming."

"They didn't want to let me in," countered Paula.

"Didn't you tell them you were James's wife?"

"Not at first," admitted Paula, feeling uncomfortable under the scrutiny of the faded blue eyes.

"Silly girl. What does it matter?" Aunt Isobel seemed to droop for a moment before she added in a softer tone of voice, "But it does matter. It once mattered to me."

"You don't mean," said Paula, suddenly struck with a completely new idea, "that you never actually married Mr. Macgregor?"

"Oh no. I married him all right. White satin and orange blossom and Mendelssohn—all the works. No. It was earlier than that that I had my dream."

Paula suddenly remembered her first meeting with Aunt Isobel.

"You wanted to study sociology," she said.

"That among other things."

At this point the nurse came in with coffee and biscuits, then put a hand on Aunt Isobel's wrist for a moment.

"Am I overtiring her?" asked Paula.

"No. I think you're doing her good."

She smiled at them both and left the room.

"I want to tell you something," said Aunt Isobel, "but I need to think first. You drink your coffee."

Paula did so, while the old woman lay with closed eyes.

"I also had ambitions to be a writer," she said presently.

"Like your brother?" suggested Paula.

"*Not* like my brother!" said Aunt Isobel very sharply. "He hated women. And I hated him."

She moved her head a little and glared at Paula. Her hands were gripping the bedclothes, her mouth was opening and closing wordlessly.

Paula, alarmed, was wondering whether to call for the

nurse, when Aunt Isobel suddenly relaxed and her face looked calm, almost tender, as if she was remembering joy.

"I wrote a play once," she said.

"Did you?" said Paula, suppressing her own excitement. "What was it about?"

"A woman of Elizabethan times, who wanted to be a writer. Shakespeare's sister, as Virginia Woolf called her in *A Room of One's Own.*"

Paula, very conscious of the torn sheets of typescript in her handbag, decided that it was best to sit quietly and listen.

"It was never published nor acted," went on Aunt Isobel in the same dreamy manner, "and nobody read it except myself and my brother. I ought never to have shown it to him." Her voice rose again and her breathing quickened.

Paula poured water into a glass and held it for her to drink.

"It doesn't matter now," said the old woman presently. "It's all so long ago and I'll soon be dead. It doesn't matter what he said. I can't even remember it, although at the time it killed me. Killed everything that mattered to me."

She closed her eyes and for several minutes there was complete silence in the room.

Paula, after checking that Aunt Isobel was breathing steadily and did not appear to be in any distress, sat down again and finished her coffee and biscuits. So that's the answer, she said to herself. I suppose I might have guessed it. She opened her handbag again and took out the torn typescript pages. She read a few words and then replaced the pages into her bag. No need to show them to Aunt Isobel now. No need to say anything at all unless Aunt Isobel herself wanted to talk. It was all too plain. The clever girl with the brilliant brother. Admiration and envy combined. She had shown him her work and he had condemned it, perhaps crudely and cruelly, perhaps with a kindly condescension that could be even worse.

Not a bad effort for a girl, but of course not to be taken seriously.

Like Mendelssohn with his musical sister. Like so many men throughout the ages.

Poor Isobel. Paula looked at the old woman, lying so quietly and peacefully now, and felt a stinging in her eyes.

But she did keep the script, Paula said to herself. Isobel kept her brainchild all these years because it was precious to her. Then somehow or other, when Uncle Mac played his cruel trick on her to unhinge her mind, it all got muddled up with her brother's books, and she must have talked in such a way as to convince others that she actually possessed an unpublished manuscript by that very famous author.

And greedy and unscrupulous people saw a chance of making money. And one of them was now dead, and another might well be dead too, and a third was on the run from a possible charge of murder.

The door opened and the nurse came in quietly.

"I think she's all right," said Paula.

"Yes, she's doing well. Her nephew is on the phone—would you like to speak to him?"

"In here? Won't I disturb her?"

"It's up to you," said the nurse.

Paula was reluctant to leave the room, but also unwilling to disturb Aunt Isobel. In the end she said, "Perhaps you'd better put it through here."

When the call came she spoke very softly. "She's sleeping at the moment, James. I won't wake her. I'll wait till you come."

"I'll be about an hour," he said.

"What's been happening?" asked Paula, though she didn't

really want to know. In her present mood the events of the last few days seemed to belong to a different world.

"The police are after Kevin," James replied. "The doctors think the old man's got a chance. Zavvy and Bridget are comforting each other, and I've had a long call from Dr. Broadbent about the results of the postmortem on Uncle Mac."

"I haven't told Auntie," murmured Paula. "Do you think I ought to?"

"I think you'd better use your own judgment," James said. "You understand her much better than I do."

"I'll do my best," promised Paula, feeling, as she so often did in spite of all their differences, a great spurt of love and gratitude for him.

When she put down the phone she saw that Aunt Isobel had woken up.

"Who was that?" she asked.

"Your nephew James."

"He's a good lad, but he still doesn't deserve you."

"Maybe I don't deserve him," said Paula.

Aunt Isobel muttered something that could have been something very Scottish and could have been something very rude. Paula decided to ignore it.

"James says he'll be here in about an hour," she said. "May I stay with you, or would you rather I went away?"

The answer was a hand stretched out to grasp Paula's.

"I'll stay," said Paula. "We don't need to talk if you don't want to, but do you think I might ask for some more coffee? I haven't had any breakfast and have had rather a busy morning."

Aunt Isobel sat up and reached for the bell. "They can bring you breakfast," she said. "James is spending a fortune on this place and I've hardly eaten anything."

Paula found herself laughing, which a few minutes ago

would have seemed out of the question. Half an hour later, after she had eaten and Aunt Isobel slept again, and the nurse had removed the tray and brought Aunt Isobel some tea, Paula decided that she ought to try to break the news about Uncle Mac. She was just planning the best way to bring up the subject when Uncle Mac's widow did it for her.

"How's the old villain? Drunk himself to death?"

"You mean Mr. Macgregor?"

"Who else?" The eyes took on the crafty expression that Paula had noticed at the dinner table when Kevin was serving them.

"I don't know whether it was actually the whisky," Paula began tentatively.

Aunt Isobel, looking more and more alert and excited, interrupted her. "He's dead!"

"Yes."

Aunt Isobel started to cough, and it turned into a fit of choking, which sounded most alarming.

Paula reached for the bell, but was stopped by a hand pulling at her wrist. She picked up the glass of water instead.

At last the choking sounds stopped, and in a surprisingly short space of time Aunt Isobel recovered enough to speak again. Her voice was weak, but there was triumph, even gloating, in it.

"So it worked. I wondered if it would. I did it, you know."

"You did—what did you do?"

Aunt Isobel told her. Paula listened intently, thinking that she ought to be horrified but in fact feeling like bursting into hysterical laughter.

It was just before James and his aunt had left the house the previous afternoon. Uncle Mac and Kevin had protested strongly about her going to the nursing home. Kevin had gone off to the summer house to sulk, and Uncle Mac had gone into his bedroom for the same reason. And to console himself with his store of Scotch.

"I poured him some of my own and took it to him myself," said Aunt Isobel. "And I said, 'Don't be silly, Mac, I'm only going because that nephew of mine insists. I'll be home in a day or two and we'll carry on as usual.'"

"And did he take the glass?"

"Yes. Why shouldn't he? He thinks I'm a silly old woman. Which often I am."

Paula ignored this. "But could it kill him so suddenly?" she asked. "He's used to whisky and he hasn't a weak heart or anything. Or has he?"

Aunt Isobel laughed again, but when another coughing fit threatened she managed to control herself.

"Of course the whisky wouldn't kill him suddenly. But I put the rest of my sleeping pills into it. There were quite a lot. I didn't know if it would work. Or if he would notice the taste. But it did work. You're looking a bit queasy, Paula. Have you eaten too quickly, or are you shocked at me?"

"I don't know, Auntie. I suppose I am shocked. I found him dead, you know. It wasn't very pleasant."

"Oh. Oh, my poor girl. Oh dear. I didn't want anything like that to happen."

She sounded genuinely distressed for the first time.

"They've done a postmortem," said Paula after a short silence. "They'll have found out what killed him."

"It doesn't matter," retorted Aunt Isobel. "They'll never know it was me. He's got lots of my pills in his cupboard."

"But the bottle—?"

"They'll never find the bottle. I brought it away with me. Which reminds me. Please give me my handbag, would you? Thanks."

Paula was not feeling at all like laughing as she watched

Aunt Isobel rummage in the bag and produce a little empty bottle.

"There you are, my dear." She handed it to Paula. "You'll get rid of it for me, won't you?"

Paula, feeling more and more uneasy, took it and put it into her bag.

Aunt Isobel lay back and gave a little sigh. "That's a weight off my mind. I'll have a rest now."

Paula stared at her. You've committed a murder, she wanted to say. But what was the point?

Aunt Isobel opened her eyes and spoke just as if she had read Paula's thoughts. "You really are shocked. I can see that. And James will be even more shocked. Very law-abiding, is James. I'm sorry you're shocked, Paula, because I like you. But I don't really care and I'm not at all sorry I did it. He deserved it."

There was a pause while she summoned up the strength to speak further.

"You feel you ought to tell the authorities. I suppose you'll have to tell them if you feel you must, but I hope you will wait till after I am dead. It won't be long now."

Paula, her mind running on sleeping pills, looked round the room.

"I've no need to take any drugs," said Aunt Isobel. "I only need another attack like last night's and I can easily bring that on myself."

Paula did not react. She was beginning to long for James to come. Her feelings towards his aunt were now such a mixture of pity and affection, shock and something like dread, that she hardly knew what to say or do. I mustn't upset her, though, she said to herself. She's quite capable of making herself ill and telling the nursing home that it's my fault. And James will never believe me and never forgive me. He hasn't the slightest idea what she is really like.

"James will be here soon," she said, looking at her watch.

"Yes," said Aunt Isobel very meekly. "I'd better rest a little so that I'm fit to talk to him."

"I wouldn't mind resting a little myself," said Paula.

There was no response, and when Paula looked at her she saw that her eyes were closed and she seemed very peaceful.

But Paula could not relax. She picked up a glossy magazine and began to turn the pages, but could find no distraction from the turmoil of her thoughts. She got up and moved quietly across to the window, looked out at the tree-lined road, and saw her own car parked very near to the entrance of the home.

Then she turned round and came back towards the bed. Something about the old woman's face caused her to ring the bell for the nurse, who came very promptly.

"Yes," said the nurse, straightening up after bending over the bed. "It won't be long now. I've seen it happen this way. It's almost as if they themselves choose the moment to die. Like animals. Very sensible."

She glanced at Paula. "Would you like to go and wait in the lounge? She won't recover consciousness now, and you look as if you could do with a break."

Paula accepted gratefully. "It's a pity her nephew didn't get here in time," she added.

"I think you'll find he'll be relieved," said the nurse, "whatever he may say."

The nurse's prophecy was fulfilled. An hour later James and Paula were sitting in the shade at the far end of their own garden and watching the cats dashing in and out of the bushes.

"I wish I could have got there in time," said James, but Paula felt sure that he didn't really mean it. His reaction to her account of the manuscript sounded much more sincere.

"Poor Aunt Isobel," he said. "I can just imagine what the

old bugger said to her. If she'd been encouraged she might have been a writer too. You read a bit of the script. What did you think of it?"

"It looked interesting. It certainly had potential."

James smiled. "Are you being tactful, love, or do you really mean that?"

"I truly believe it, from the little I saw."

"A wasted talent. A wasted life. A bastard of a brother and a bastard of a husband. At least I never had to show her that letter of Mac's."

"No. That's a blessing."

They were silent for a little while, relishing the peace and comfort of their home.

Then James said, "Odd that he chose the very drug she was taking to mix with the whisky for his suicide brew."

"Sorry," said Paula. "What did you say? I think I must have fallen asleep for a moment."

James explained in detail. "He kept a good supply of her sleeping pills in his cupboard and handed them out when needed."

"And that was all?" asked Paula. "I mean, there wasn't any other drug present?"

"That was all, but together with the alcohol it was enough. Of course he'd know about that, with his pharmacy experience."

"So there'll be no doubt about the verdict when it comes to the inquest?"

"No doubt at all. Together with the letter, it's very conclusive. There's only one thing that's rather odd," added James.

"What's that?"

"The bottle that contained the pills. What did he do with it?"

It's in my handbag, was Paula's unspoken reply.

"There wasn't any bottle in the room when I found him," she said aloud.

"Exactly. He must have had the pills loose somewhere, or in another container. Maybe he kept them easily accessible. Or maybe Auntie left her own behind and after we'd gone he fetched them from her room."

"There'd have been a bottle then," said Paula.

"Yes, of course. But in any case it can't have been like that, because she brought all her medicines with her and gave them to the matron."

"You're sure about that?"

"Pretty sure. I didn't actually see her do it," added James. "I didn't want her to feel we didn't trust her. She'd had enough of that sort of thing from her husband."

"Oh well," said Paula, yawning, "I don't suppose it will make any difference to the verdict."

"No, that's a foregone conclusion," said James. "The facts are plain enough. Where are you going?"

"I'm going to make us some lunch."

"Shall I come and help?"

"No thanks. I won't be long."

Paula walked slowly across the lawn. A little bottle, she was saying to herself, how does one get rid of it? I'll have to do it at once. The dustmen come tomorrow morning early. I'll mix it in with the rest of the rubbish. That's the simplest and the safest. I only wish I could dispose of my own conscience so easily.

DISCOVER THE ACCLAIMED NOVELS FROM AWARD-WINNING AUTHOR

PETER ROBINSON

Praise for the mysteries of Peter Robinson and his astounding British detective, Chief Inspector Alan Banks

__THE HANGING VALLEY 0-425-14196-9/$4.99

"Powerful...highly recommended."—The Kirkus Reviews

"This roller-coaster plot hurtles toward a surprising and satisfying climax."—Booklist

__PAST REASON HATED 0-425-14489-5/$5.99

"Intriguing...surprising...satisfying."—Booklist

"Proves the equal of legends of the genre such as P. D. James and Ruth Rendell."—St. Louis Post-Dispatch

"An expert plotter with an eye for telling detail."

—New York Times Book Review

__FINAL ACCOUNT 0-425-14935-8/$21.95

"Robinson's skill with the British police procedural has been burnished to a high gloss."—Chicago Tribune

A Berkley Prime Crime hardcover

Payable in U.S. funds. No cash orders accepted. Postage & handling: $1.75 for one book, 75¢ for each additional. Maximum postage $5.50. Prices, postage and handling charges may change without notice. Visa, Amex, MasterCard call 1-800-788-6262, ext. 1, refer to ad # 524a

Or, check above books and send this order form to:
The Berkley Publishing Group
390 Murray Hill Pkwy., Dept. B
East Rutherford, NJ 07073

Bill my: ☐ Visa ☐ MasterCard ☐ Amex ______ (expires)

Card#______________________ ($15 minimum)

Signature______________________

Please allow 6 weeks for delivery. **Or enclosed is my:** ☐ check ☐ money order

Name______________________ Book Total $______

Address______________________ Postage & Handling $______

City______________________ Applicable Sales Tax $______ (NY, NJ, PA, CA, GST Can.)

State/ZIP______________________ Total Amount Due $______

"Albert's characters are as real and quirky as your next-door neighbor."—Raleigh News & Observer

SUSAN WITTIG ALBERT

__THYME OF DEATH 0-425-14098-9/$4.99

"A wonderful character...smart, real, and totally a woman of the nineties."—*Mostly Murder*

China Bayles left her law practice to open an herb shop in Pecan Springs, Texas. But tensions run high in small towns, too—and the results can be murder.

__WITCHES' BANE 0-425-14406-2/$5.50

"A delightful cast of unusual characters...entertaining and engaging."—*Booklist*

When a series of Halloween pranks turn deadly, China must investigate to unmask a killer.

__HANGMAN'S ROOT 0-425-14898-X/$5.50

"The plot unfolds briskly and with sly humor."
—*Publishers Weekly*

When a prominent animal researcher is murdered, China discovers a fervent animal rights activist isn't the only person who wanted him dead.

Now available in Prime Crime hardcover

__ROSEMARY REMEMBERED 0-425-14937-4/$19.95

When Rosemary Robbins, a woman who looks just like China, is found murdered in a pick-up truck, China takes the advice of a psychic and looks for a killer close to home.

Payable in U.S. funds. No cash orders accepted. Postage & handling: $1.75 for one book, 75¢ for each additional. Maximum postage $5.50. Prices, postage and handling charges may change without notice. Visa, Amex, MasterCard call 1-800-788-6262, ext. 1, refer to ad # 546a

Or, check above books and send this order form to:
The Berkley Publishing Group
390 Murray Hill Pkwy., Dept. B
East Rutherford, NJ 07073
Please allow 6 weeks for delivery.

Bill my: ☐ Visa ☐ MasterCard ☐ Amex ______ (expires)

Card#______________________ ($15 minimum)

Signature______________________

Or enclosed is my: ☐ check ☐ money order

Name______________________ Book Total $______

Address______________________ Postage & Handling $______

City______________________ Applicable Sales Tax $______
(NY, NJ, PA, CA, GST Can.)

State/ZIP______________________ Total Amount Due $______

EARLENE FOWLER

Introduces Benni Harper, curator of San Celina's folk art museum and amateur sleuth

"Benni's loose, friendly, and bright. Here's hoping we get to see more of her..."–The Kirkus Reviews

__FOOL'S PUZZLE 0-425-14545-X/$4.99

Ex-cowgirl Benni Harper moved to San Celina, California, to begin a new career as curator of the town's folk art museum. But when one of the museum's first quilt exhibit artists is found dead, Benni must piece together a pattern of family secrets and small-town lies to catch the killer.

__IRISH CHAIN 0-425-15137-9/$5.50

When Brady O'Hara and his former girlfriend are murdered at the San Celina Senior Citizen's Prom, Benni believes it's more than mere jealousy. She risks everything–her exhibit, her romance with police chief Gabriel Ortiz, and her life–to unveil the conspiracy O'Hara had been hiding for fifty years.

__KANSAS TROUBLES 0-425-15148-4/$19.95

After their wedding, Benni and Gabe visit his hometown near Wichita. There Benni meets Tyler Brown: aspiring country singer, gifted quilter, and former Amish wife. But when Tyler is murdered and the case comes between Gabe and her, Benni learns that her marriage is much like the Kansas weather: unexpected and bound to be stormy.

A Prime Crime Hardcover

Payable in U.S. funds. No cash orders accepted. Postage & handling: $1.75 for one book, 75¢ for each additional. Maximum postage $5.50. Prices, postage and handling charges may change without notice. Visa, Amex, MasterCard call 1-800-788-6262, ext. 1, refer to ad # 523b

Or, check above books and send this order form to:
The Berkley Publishing Group
390 Murray Hill Pkwy., Dept. B
East Rutherford, NJ 07073

Bill my: ☐ Visa ☐ MasterCard ☐ Amex ______ (expires)

Card#________________________ ($15 minimum)

Signature________________________

Please allow 6 weeks for delivery. **Or enclosed is my:** ☐ check ☐ money order

Name________________________ Book Total $______

Address________________________ Postage & Handling $______

City________________________ Applicable Sales Tax $______ (NY, NJ, PA, CA, GST Can.)

State/ZIP________________________ Total Amount Due $______

Featuring Bill Hawley, a funeral director who comforts mourners—and catches murderers. Because sometimes the death certificate doesn't tell the whole story...

LEO AXLER

__DOUBLE PLOT 0-425-14407-0/$4.50

When an accidental crash begins to look like suicide, Bill Hawley reluctantly agrees to take the case. And he soon discovers the man's life was as fake as his death.

__FINAL VIEWING 0-425-14244-2/$4.50

A newly widowed woman finds the story of her husband's death suspicious, and she puts Bill Hawley on the case to make sure the truth isn't buried with the body.

__GRAVE MATTERS 0-425-14581-6/$4.99

When a man is killed from multiple dog bites, a mysterious midnight message leads Bill Hawley into the dangerous underworld of illegal dog fighting.

__SEPARATED BY DEATH 0-425-15257-X/$5.50

Bill Hawley has found more than just a body in a newly arrived coffin. Also hidden inside is the severed head of a woman—embalmed, surgically removed, and impossible to identify.

Payable in U.S. funds. No cash orders accepted. Postage & handling: $1.75 for one book, 75¢ for each additional. Maximum postage $5.50. Prices, postage and handling charges may change without notice. Visa, Amex, MasterCard call 1-800-788-6262, ext. 1, refer to ad # 635a

Or, check above books and send this order form to: **Bill my:** ☐ Visa ☐ MasterCard ☐ Amex ______ (expires)

The Berkley Publishing Group Card#______________ ($15 minimum)
390 Murray Hill Pkwy., Dept. B
East Rutherford, NJ 07073 Signature______________

Please allow 6 weeks for delivery. **Or enclosed is my:** ☐ check ☐ money order

Name______________ Book Total $______

Address______________ Postage & Handling $______

City______________ Applicable Sales Tax $______
(NY, NJ, PA, CA, GST Can.)

State/ZIP______________ Total Amount Due $______